TODOS SANTOS

By Susan Smith Nash

TODOS SANTOS

ISBN: print 978-1-945784-15-6
ISBN: ebook 978-1-945784-16-3

Texture Press
1609 Oklahoma Avenue
Norman, OK 73071

"We are consciousness learning to recognize itself in forms that existence has never contained before."

Setting: Todos Santos, Baja California, Mexico; Norman, Oklahoma; Texas Panhandle
Themes: Grief, resurrection, consciousness evolution, existentialism, social construction of reality, abjection
Genre: Literary science fiction with philosophical and horror elements

Printed in the United States of America.

Acknowledgments

Thank you to everyone who supported the development of this story, including readers, editors, and all those who believe in the transformative power of narrative.

TABLE OF CONTENTS

PART III: TRANSFORMATION

PART IV: RESURRECTION

CHARACTER GUIDE

WISTERIA VANISH - 32, protagonist. Former competitive swimmer, psychology PhD specializing in trauma. Lost husband David to IED in Afghanistan. Writes poetry, drives Jeep with "SWIMMER" plates.

DR. HOLDSBY ASHER - 38, "The Medic." Former Army combat medic, expelled from medical school for unauthorized stem cell research. Mixed Anglo-Hispanic heritage, operates laboratory in abandoned mine.

ELENA - Age unknown, resurrected trafficking victim who becomes conscious and claims agency. Develops into consciousness evolution coordinator.

JACKSON REEVES - 45, "The Extortionist." VitaNuova contractor, former Navy SEAL. Collects vintage fountain pens, writes threatening notes by hand.

MARIA BENTLEY - 55, hotel owner. Former British pharmaceutical researcher hiding from scientific fraud charges.

DAVID TORRES - Deceased, Wisteria's husband. Staff Sergeant killed by IED in Afghanistan. Appears as consciousness pattern in liminal space.

PHILOSOPHICAL THEMES

Existentialism: Sartre's radical freedom, Camus's absurd hero, Kierkegaard's leap of faith, existence preceding essence

Social Construction of Reality: Berger and Luckmann's ideas about how society determines what counts as "real" and who counts as "human"

Abjection: Julia Kristeva's concept of horror at boundary dissolution; beings existing between categories

Consciousness Evolution: Exploration of identity as performance vs. essence; individual vs. collective awareness

Trauma and Healing: Moving from adaptation to transformation; collective support transcending individual limitation

---

GEOGRAPHIC SETTINGS

Norman, Oklahoma: University town; Wisteria's home base with aquatic center and therapy practice

Texas Panhandle: Vast High Plains landscape; philosophical emptiness and geological time

Amarillo, Texas: Corporate meeting point; crossroads decision-making

Baja California: Desert meeting ocean; Sonoran Desert ecosystem with cardón cacti, ocotillo, palo verde

Todos Santos: "All Saints" - colonial Mexican town transformed into artist colony and consciousness evolution center

Sierra de la Laguna: Mountain range housing abandoned silver mine laboratory

Pacific Ocean: Infinite horizon representing consciousness possibilities; salt water connecting all existence

---

CHAPTER 1: SALT AND MEMORY

"The future stretched before them like an ocean of possibility, infinite in its potential for exploration, patient in its willingness to support whatever forms consciousness might choose to become."

The pool at the Norman Aquatic Center held Wisteria Vanish's secrets the way desert sand holds water—reluctantly, but completely. At 5:30 AM, the chlorinated silence wrapped around her like a familiar embrace as she sliced through lanes marked by faded plastic ropes. Her platinum blonde hair, darkened by water, was held tight to her head by an aqua blue silicone Speedo swim cap.

Stroke. Stroke. Stroke. Breathe.

The rhythm had saved her sanity for thirty-two years, through her mother's manic episodes and subsequent hospitalizations, through her doctoral dissertation on trauma psychology, through the worst phone call of her life eighteen months ago. The one that began, "Mrs. Vanish, I regret to inform you that Staff Sergeant David Torres..."

Wisteria touched the pool's edge with fingertips that had once been strong enough to slice through water at collegiate championship speeds. Now they trembled slightly as she hauled herself from the water, her lean frame still carrying the broad shoulders and narrow hips of a serious swimmer. The morning sun, filtering through the aquatic center's skylights, caught the water droplets on her skin like tiny prisms.

Her mother had named her Wisteria because she thought it would sound poetic with their unusual surname—Wisteria Vanish, like something that might disappear in the wind or bloom unexpectedly against a garden wall. "Names have power, you know," her mother had said during one of her lucid periods between hospitalizations. "They tell the world who you might become."

Wisteria did not quite believe her. She thought her mother used her name like an incantation.

Oklahoma in early September still held summer's grip, the air thick with humidity that made the approaching autumn feel like a distant promise. Wisteria wrapped herself in a her favorite thick terry towel—the same one she'd used since graduate school—and padded barefoot across the concrete deck. The familiar scent of chlorine and the slapping of her flip-flops in the empty space provided a cocoon of normalcy she desperately needed.

Her phone buzzed against the metal bench where she'd left it. Wisteria's stomach clenched. Early morning calls never brought good news. She'd learned that lesson the hard way.

"Dr. Vanish?" The voice was crisp, professional, with the hint of an East Coast accent.

"This is Wisteria."

"My name is Harrison Webb. I represent VitaNuova, Incorporated. We have a proposition that might interest you."

Wisteria's grip tightened on the phone. VitaNuova—she'd heard the name whispered in academic circles, usually followed by raised eyebrows and uncomfortable silences. Biotech defense contractor. The name was darkly ironic, considering their work: "New Life," like Dante's poem about rebirth and redemption, but applied to military applications that had nothing to do with spiritual renewal.

"I'm not looking for new clients right now," she said, pulling off her swim cap with her free hand and gathering up her swim bag to head into the showers.

"This isn't about therapy, Dr. Vanish. We need someone with your particular background to investigate some... unusual developments in Mexico. Specifically, in Baja California."

Through the aquatic center's windows, Wisteria could see the University of Oklahoma campus stirring to life. Students with backpacks crossed the quad, their voices carrying across the morning air. Normal life. Safe life. The kind of life she'd built carefully around her grief like a levee against flood waters.

"What kind of developments?"

Webb's pause lasted a heartbeat too long. "The kind that might interest someone who's lost someone important to warfare."

Wisteria's breath caught. The pool deck seemed to tilt beneath her feet.

Her first reaction was an overwhelming rush of impotent rage. It would not do any good to let this stranger know, however. So, she controlled her voice.

"How do you know about David?"

"We know about a lot of things, Dr. Vanish. Including your mother's condition, your dissertation on battlefield trauma, and your current client base of veterans with PTSD. You understand loss. You understand how far people will go to avoid it."

The towel slipped from Wisteria's hands. Around her, the pool's surface had settled into perfect stillness, reflecting the overhead lights like fallen stars.

"I'm listening."

"There's a man in Todos Santos, Mexico. A former combat medic named Holdsby Asher. He's been making claims about reversing death. Bringing back the recently deceased. Our sources suggest he might actually be succeeding."

Wisteria's mind raced through the scientific impossibilities, the ethical violations, the sheer audacity of such a claim. But underneath her rational dismissal, something else stirred—a desperate hope she'd thought she'd buried with David.

"That's impossible."

"Is it? You're a trauma specialist, Dr. Vanish. You know that the line between life and death isn't always as clear as we'd like to believe. Sometimes it's more like a border that can be... well, for all intents and purposes, crossed."

The morning sun had climbed higher, sending long shadows across the pool deck. Wisteria watched a maintenance worker drag a net through the water, collecting leaves that had fallen overnight. Such a simple task—removing the debris, keeping the water clean. If only healing worked the same way.

"What exactly are you asking me to do?"

"Go to Todos Santos. Evaluate this Holdsby Asher. Determine if his methods have any scientific basis. If they do..." Webb's voice took on a different quality, softer but somehow more dangerous. "If they do, we'd like to discuss a partnership."

Wisteria made her way into the empty locker room. Her reflection stared back at her from the mirror above the sinks around the corner from the showers. There she was—hollow-eyed, blonde hair falling in damp tangles, wearing the expression of someone who'd been treading water for too long. She thought of David's last letter, still unopened in her bedroom drawer. She thought of her mother, who'd spent Wisteria's childhood disappearing into the locked wards of state hospitals, always chasing the promise of a cure that never came.

"I'll need time to think about it."

"Of course. But Dr. Vanish?" Webb's voice carried a note of gentle insistence. "Don't think too long. Some opportunities have expiration dates."

The line went dead. Wisteria stood motionless in the locker room, thinking about the neat, even swim lanes where life's chaos could be held at bay, even if only in the absence of external intrusions while swimming. No text messages, no news feeds, no unwelcome calls – at least while swimming laps. Now, she had to face something unexpected. She'd spent her life studying the psychology of trauma, helping others navigate the landscape of loss. But she'd never imagined that someone might offer her a map back to the country of the living.

Her phone buzzed again. A text message from her assistant: "Your 9 AM canceled. Mrs. Patterson's husband had another episode."

Wisteria looked at her watch: 7:15 AM. Time enough to drive home, change into clothes for work, and prepare for a day of helping others manage their grief while her own remained a constant, gnawing presence. She gathered her things, her movements automatic from years of the same routine.

But as she walked toward the parking lot, Wisteria's reflection followed her in the aquatic center's windows—a woman suspended between water and air, between the life she'd built and the life she'd lost, between the rational world of psychology and the impossible promise of resurrection.

The Oklahoma sky stretched endless above her, the color of David's eyes in morning light. Wisteria unlocked her Jeep and sat behind the wheel, key in the ignition but engine silent. Around her, the world continued its normal rotation, but she felt herself

19

standing at the edge of something vast and unknowable, like a swimmer preparing for a dive into dark water.

She thought of her mother's journal, filled with poetry written during manic episodes—beautiful, terrible verses about drowning and flying, about the thin membrane between sanity and madness. Wisteria had inherited that gift for words, though she'd learned to channel it into sonnets instead of symptoms.

What if the dead could speak? she'd written in her own journal the night after David's funeral. *What would they say to those who remain?*

Now, sitting in her Jeep in the parking lot of the Norman Aquatic Center, Wisteria wondered if she was about to find out.

CHAPTER 2: THE PANHANDLE SKY

The highway stretched before Wisteria like a gray ribbon thrown across the vastness of the Texas Panhandle, disappearing into a horizon that seemed to exist in another dimension entirely. Interstate 40 cut through landscape so flat and endless that it challenged the human brain's ability to process scale—mile after mile of grassland punctuated by the occasional pump jacks, their mechanical heads nodding like giant metal birds drinking from the earth's hidden reserves.

Wisteria had left Norman before dawn, her Jeep loaded with a single duffel bag and a leather portfolio containing her credentials, passport, and a cashier's check from VitaNuova, Inc. for more money than she'd made in the past two years combined. The check had arrived by courier within hours of her acceptance call, along with detailed travel arrangements and a brief dossier on Dr. Holdsby Asher that read like a military record with half the pages redacted.

Now, three hours into the drive, the Oklahoma hills had given way to the geological democracy of the High Plains—a landscape that had once been seafloor, then grassland, then dustbowl, then grassland again. The earth here held memory in its sedimentary layers: ancient oceans, vast subtropical swamps, extensive deserts laying down redbeds, and then, in the time between the last ice ages and now, buffalo herds, failed wheat farms, and the dreams of people who'd tried to make something permanent in a place that specialized in impermanence.

Wisteria pulled off at a truck stop outside Amarillo, her back stiff from the drive and her mind churning with questions she'd been trying to avoid. The facility sprawled across several acres—diesel pumps, a convenience store, a restaurant that promised "World's Best Chicken Fried Steak," and a parking lot filled with eighteen-wheelers whose drivers were catching sleep in their cabs before the next leg of their journeys.

The bathroom mirror showed her what the early morning and long drive had accomplished: blonde hair escaping from its ponytail, blue eyes that carried more shadow than usual, the kind of pallor that came from too little sleep and too much caffeine. She splashed cold water on her face and tried to recognize the woman staring back at her.

When had she become someone who would accept money to investigate impossible claims? When had grief made her desperate enough to chase fairy tales across state lines?

The answer, she knew, was exactly eighteen months, two weeks, and three days ago.

"Ma'am? You okay?"

Wisteria turned to find a woman in her sixties watching her with concern. She wore a Desert Storm Veteran cap and a denim jacket covered in military patches. Her face had the weathered quality of someone who'd spent years outdoors, and her eyes held the particular alertness Wisteria recognized in her veteran clients.

"I'm fine," Wisteria said, then amended, "I'm tired. Long drive."

"Where you headed?"

"Mexico. Baja California."

The woman raised an eyebrow. "That's a hell of a drive. You got family down there?"

Wisteria hesitated. How to explain that she was chasing the possibility of resurrection? That a defense contractor had offered her enough money to investigate a man who claimed he could bring back the dead?

"Work," she said finally.

"What kind of work takes a woman like you to Mexico?" The question wasn't hostile, just curious. Wisteria sensed the protective instinct of someone who'd seen too many people make dangerous choices. "I would have hoped it was a nice, relaxing (or exhausting) vacation with family."

"I'm a psychologist. Trauma specialist."

"Ah." The woman nodded as if that explained everything. "Military?"

"Some of my clients are veterans, yes."

"Lose someone over there?"

The question hit Wisteria like a physical blow. She gripped the edge of the sink, knuckles white against the porcelain.

"I'm sorry," the woman said immediately. "That was out of line. I just... I can tell. You got that look."

"What look?"

"The look of someone who's still fighting a war that ended for everyone else."

Wisteria studied the woman's face in the mirror. "You lost someone too."

"My husband. Marine. Second tour in Afghanistan." The woman's voice remained steady, but her hands trembled slightly as she adjusted her cap. "IED outside Kandahar. Three years ago last month."

They stood in silence for a moment, two women in a truck stop bathroom sharing the particular grief of those left behind by war. Wisteria thought of the support groups she'd facilitated, the careful language of healing and acceptance she'd learned to deploy like verbal medication. But standing here, she found herself wordless.

"The thing is," the woman continued, "you reach a point where you'd do anything to have them back. Even for five minutes. Even if it meant making a deal with the devil himself."

Wisteria's phone buzzed. A text from an unknown number: *Flight leaves at 6 PM tomorrow evening. Meeting ahead of that. Will send details. - HW*

"I have to go," Wisteria said.

"Be careful down there, honey. Mexico's not what it used to be, especially for Americans traveling alone."

Wisteria nodded and headed for the door, then turned back. "What was your husband's name?"

"Marcus. Marcus Williams. He wanted to be a teacher when he got back. History."

"I'm sorry for your loss."

"I'm sorry for yours too, honey. And whatever you're chasing down there... just remember that some doors, once you open them, you can't close again."

Wisteria left the truck stop with the woman's words echoing in her mind. She drove through Shamrock as the sun reached its zenith, the small town shimmering in heat waves that made the Dairy Queen she planned to visit shimmer a bit. The Texas Panhandle stretched endlessly around her—a landscape so vast it made human concerns seem microscopic, yet somehow managed to amplify the weight of individual loss.

She stopped for gas at a station where tumbleweeds had collected against the fence like nature's version of chain-link snow. As she filled her tank, Wisteria watched a red-tailed hawk circle overhead, riding thermals in slow, mesmerizing spirals. The bird moved with the kind of patience that came from understanding that persistence, not speed, was the key to survival in harsh country.

Her phone rang. Dr. Chen, her therapist. To keep herself grounded, Wisteria continued to see a therapist once a month, at minimum.

"Wisteria, I got your message. Are you sure about this trip?"

"I'm already in Texas."

"That's not what I asked."

Wisteria leaned against her Jeep, watching traffic flow past on the interstate. "I have to do this, Linda. I can't explain why, but I have to."

"This sounds like magical thinking. You know that, right? The idea that this man in Mexico might have some way to—"

"I know how it sounds."

"Do you? Because it sounds like a woman in the acute phase of grief making decisions that could put her in danger."

Wisteria closed her eyes. Dr. Chen was right, of course. Everything about this trip violated the principles of healthy grief processing. She was chasing an impossible hope, funded by people whose motives she barely understood, toward a destination that might not offer anything but further loss.

"What if it's not impossible?" Wisteria asked quietly.

"Wisteria—"

"What if there's something we don't understand about death? About the line between life and whatever comes after? What if science is just finally catching up to what people have always hoped was true?"

The silence stretched between them across hundreds of miles.

"I can't stop you," Dr. Chen said finally. "But I want you to promise me something. If this starts to feel dangerous—and I mean any kind of danger, physical or psychological—you'll come home."

"I promise."

"And Wisteria? Keep writing. In your journal. Poetry, whatever. Keep processing what you experience. Don't let yourself get lost in someone else's story."

After hanging up, Wisteria sat in her Jeep for a long moment, engine running, air conditioning fighting against the Texas heat. Around her, the Panhandle continued its ancient routine—wind moving across grass, clouds casting shadows that raced across the plains, the steady rhythm of a landscape that had witnessed countless human dramas and remained essentially unchanged.

She thought of her last poem, written the night before she'd accepted VitaNuova's offer:

The dead have no country
But the living build borders
Around their absence,
Checkpoint grief
Where memory must show
Its papers
To pass.

She read the lines again, and her face reddened a bit. "It's a dumb idea for a poem. Too tidy."

The Amarillo airport was still fairly far away. Wisteria pulled back onto the interstate, her Jeep a small speck moving across the immensity of the High Plains. In her rearview mirror, the truck stop dwindled to a distant cluster of lights, and she wondered if she'd ever see this landscape again—or if she'd ever again be the woman who was seeing it now.

The radio played country music that spoke of heartbreak and redemption, of people making bad choices for good reasons. Wisteria changed channels to a political commentator who energized himself through outrage and pressed harder on the accelerator, chasing the horizon toward whatever waited for her in the desert by the sea.

CHAPTER 3: CROSSROADS IN AMARILLO

The Marriott in Amarillo rose from the plains like a geometric anomaly, its glass and steel facade reflecting the endless Texas sky in fractured segments. Wisteria sat in the hotel restaurant, drinking a club soda, no ice, pushing her salad around on the plate, and watching the sun set through floor-to-ceiling windows that framed the horizon like a painting. The meeting with VitaNuova's representatives wasn't until tomorrow, but she'd arrived early, needing time to process the enormity of what she was considering.

The restaurant was populated by the usual mix of business travelers and locals—men in crisp shirts discussing quarterly reports, women in professional attire checking phones between sips of wine. Wisteria felt like an anthropologist observing a species she'd once belonged to but could no longer fully understand. When had normal life become so foreign to her?

"Dr. Vanish?"

Wisteria turned to find a woman approaching her table—mid-forties, auburn hair pulled back in a neat chignon, wearing a charcoal suit that managed to be both professional and approachable. She moved with the confident stride of someone accustomed to command.

"I'm Rebecca Walsh, VitaNuova's Director of Special Projects. I hope you don't mind that I'm here now. I was hoping we could have an informal conversation before tomorrow's briefing."

Wisteria gestured to the empty chair across from her. "Please, sit."

Rebecca ordered a glass of Pinot Grigio and studied Wisteria with intelligent green eyes. "You're not what I expected."

"What did you expect?"

"Someone harder. More desperate. The kind of person who'd jump at an opportunity like this without asking questions."

"Should I be flattered or concerned?"

Rebecca smiled. "Both, probably. The truth is, Dr. Vanish, we need someone with your specific combination of skills and... motivation. Someone who understands trauma psychology but also has personal investment in the outcome."

"You mean someone who's lost someone to war."

"I mean someone who's lost someone they loved to circumstances beyond their control. Someone who might be willing to take risks that others wouldn't."

Wisteria sipped her club soda, buying time to think. Through the window, she could see the lights of Amarillo beginning to twinkle against the deepening sky. Somewhere out there, trucks were moving along the interstate, carrying goods and people toward destinations unknown. The world continued its relentless forward motion while she sat suspended between her past and an uncertain future.

"Tell me about Holdsby Asher."

Rebecca reached into her briefcase and withdrew a tablet, swiping to bring up a file. "Dr. Holdsby Asher, age thirty-eight. Born in Albuquerque, New Mexico. Mixed heritage—his father was Anglo, his mother from a prominent Hispanic family with roots going back to the colonial period. Outstanding student, full scholarship to Johns Hopkins for pre-med. Enlisted in the Army after 9/11, became a combat medic with the 82nd Airborne."

She swiped to a military photograph—a younger Holdsby in dress uniform, eyes clear and determined, the hint of a smile playing at the corners of his mouth. Wisteria felt an unexpected flutter of recognition, as if she were looking at someone she'd known in another life.

"Three tours in Afghanistan, two in Iraq. Silver Star, Bronze Star with V Device, Purple Heart. By all accounts, an exemplary soldier and medic. Saved dozens of lives under fire."

"What happened?"

Rebecca's expression darkened. "His unit was ambushed outside Fallujah in 2010. Asher was the only survivor. He spent six months in military hospitals, then was medically discharged with PTSD and traumatic brain injury. The Army offered him full disability, but he refused it. Said he was going back to medical school."

"Did he?"

"Johns Hopkins again. Full scholarship. Top of his class for two years, then..." Rebecca paused, seeming to choose her words carefully. "Then he began conducting unauthorized research. Experiments involving stem cells and tissue regeneration. When the university found out, they expelled him and threatened criminal charges."

Wisteria felt a chill that had nothing to do with the air conditioning. "What kind of experiments?"

"The kind that suggested he was trying to reverse death itself."

The bar around them continued its normal rhythms—conversations about business deals and weekend plans, the clink of glasses, the soft jazz playing through hidden speakers. But Wisteria felt as if she and Rebecca were sitting in a bubble of silence, discussing impossibilities while the world remained obliviously normal.

"That was four years ago," Rebecca continued. "He disappeared from the medical community entirely. We lost track of him until recently, when our sources in Mexico began reporting strange stories from Todos Santos. Stories about a gringo doctor who could bring back the dead."

"Stories."

"At first, yes. But then we started getting more specific reports. Names of people who'd been declared dead and were walking around town days later. Medical records that didn't match observable reality. Videos that are... difficult to explain."

Rebecca swiped to a grainy video file on her tablet. Wisteria leaned forward, squinting at the low-resolution footage. It showed what appeared to be a medical examination room, stark white walls and bright overhead lighting. A figure lay on a gurney, clearly deceased—skin gray, eyes closed, the absolute stillness that only comes with death.

Then the figure moved.

Wisteria's breath caught. "That could be faked."

"It could be. But we have seventeen similar videos from different sources. Some show the same subjects weeks later, apparently healthy and mobile."

"Apparently."

"Yes. That's the key word. Our sources suggest that while these individuals appear to be alive, they're... different. Changed. They don't speak, don't seem to respond to normal stimuli. They move and breathe, but they're not exactly alive in any sense we'd recognize."

Wisteria thought of her mother, during the worst of her manic episodes, when she'd seemed to be possessed by something that wasn't quite human. The way she'd move without purpose, speak without meaning, as if the essential spark that made her *her* had temporarily departed.

"What does VitaNuova want with this?"

Rebecca's smile was sharp. "We're a biotech defense contractor, Dr. Vanish. We're always interested in innovations that might give our clients an advantage. Imagine soldiers who couldn't be killed, or at least couldn't stay dead. Imagine the tactical applications."

"Imagine the ethical implications."

"Ethics are a luxury we can't always afford. Not when American lives are at stake."

Wisteria finished her club soda and made eye contact with the waitstaff for another. Around them, the restaurant was filling with the dinner crowd—couples sharing appetizers, business groups gathered around high-top tables. Normal people living normal lives, unaware that two women were discussing the possibility of conquering death itself.

"Why me?" Wisteria asked. "You could send a team of military doctors, scientists with more relevant expertise."

"Because Asher won't talk to them. He's paranoid, suspicious of anyone with obvious government connections. But you..." Rebecca gestured with her wine glass. "You're a trauma psychologist. A civilian. Someone who understands loss on a personal level. Someone he might trust."

"And if I determine that his methods are legitimate?"

"Then we move to phase two. Full scientific evaluation, with your assistance. If the technology can be reproduced and controlled, we'd want to bring it back to the United States for further development."

Wisteria stared out the window at the lights of Amarillo, thinking of all the people in this city who'd lost someone they loved. Parents who'd buried children, spouses who'd said goodbye to partners, children who'd watched parents fade away. How many of them would give anything for a second chance?

"And if I determine that it's not legitimate?"

Rebecca's expression became carefully neutral. "Then you come home, and we pay you for your time."

"What aren't you telling me?"

"I'm sorry?"

"There's something else. Something you're not saying."

Rebecca was quiet for a long moment, swirling the wine in her glass. "Asher has been making threats. Against American interests, against the military establishment that he believes failed him. We have reason to believe he might be planning something... destructive."

"Such as?"

"We're not sure. But a man with his capabilities and his grudges could cause significant damage if he chose to."

Wisteria felt the familiar weight of being asked to help fix someone else's broken pieces while her own remained scattered. But underneath her professional skepticism, hope continued to flutter like a trapped bird.

"I'll need complete access to his facility, his research, his methods."

"Of course."

"And I'll need guarantees about my safety. Mexico can be dangerous for Americans, especially those involved in sensitive research."

"We'll provide security support. Discreet, but effective."

Wisteria nodded slowly. "I'll give you my answer tomorrow morning."

Rebecca smiled and raised her glass. "To second chances, Dr. Vanish."

Wisteria raised her club soda in response, though she didn't echo the toast. As she watched Rebecca Walsh disappear into the elevator, she wondered if she was about to make the best decision of her life or the worst one.

That night, in her hotel room overlooking the Texas Panhandle, Wisteria sat at the small desk and opened her leather journal. The blank page stared back at her, waiting for words that might make sense of the impossible choice she faced.

Finally, she wrote:

At the crossroads where hope meets desperation,
Where grief builds altars
To gods who promise
What science cannot deliver,
I stand
Counting the cost
Of believing
In resurrection.

Outside her window, the lights of Amarillo stretched toward the horizon, each one representing someone who'd made their own choice between acceptance and rebellion, between the safety of known sorrow and the dangerous possibility of joy.

Wisteria closed her journal and reached for her phone. She had a call to make.

CHAPTER 4: THE MEDIC'S INTRODUCTION

The turbulence hit as Wisteria's flight descended through storm clouds toward Los Cabos International Airport, the small regional jet bucking and shuddering like a bronco trying to throw its rider. Wisteria gripped the armrests of her window seat, watching lightning fracture the darkness beyond the rain-streaked glass. The plane dropped suddenly, leaving her stomach somewhere above her head, and she closed her eyes, trying to find the calm center that had carried her through years of competitive swimming.

Breathe in for four counts, hold for four, breathe out for four.

The meditation technique had been her mother's gift—one of the few useful things she'd learned during her stays in psychiatric facilities. "When the world gets too loud," her mother had whispered during one of her lucid moments, "you find the quiet place inside yourself and swim there."

"Señorita, are you alright?"

Wisteria opened her eyes to find the man across the aisle watching her with concern. He was younger than she'd initially thought—mid-thirties, with dark hair and eyes that seemed to hold depths she couldn't quite fathom. His features suggested mixed heritage—the sharp cheekbones and olive complexion that spoke of Native American and Hispanic ancestry, combined with the angular jaw line of Northern European stock.

"I'm fine," she said, though her knuckles were white against the armrest. "Just not a fan of turbulence."

"Qué vuelo. Qué suerte que llegamos vivos," he said with a slight smile. "What a flight. Lucky we got here alive."

Wisteria found herself studying his face in the intermittent flashes of lightning. There was something familiar about him, though she was certain they'd never met. His features were sharp but not harsh, and his eyes held the particular alertness she recognized in her veteran clients—the look of someone who'd learned to scan for danger even in safe situations. A turquoise-and-silver bracelet caught the cabin light as he adjusted his position.

"¿Y así somos?" she found herself asking. "Are we?"

His smile widened, revealing straight white teeth. "That's a philosophical question. What constitutes being alive? Breathing? Thinking? Feeling? Or something else entirely?"

The plane lurched again, and Wisteria felt her stomach rebel. She pressed her hand to her mouth, fighting nausea.

"Here." The man reached into his carry-on bag and withdrew a small packet. "Crystallized ginger wedges. They help with motion sickness."

"Thank you." Wisteria accepted the packet, noting that his fingers were long and steady—surgeon's hands, or perhaps a musician's. A faint scar ran along his left index finger. "Are you a doctor?"

"I was, once. Now I'm... something else."

The plane's descent steepened, and through the window Wisteria could see the lights of Los Cabos appearing through breaks in the storm clouds. The city spread along the coast like scattered jewels, the sea beyond it lost in darkness.

"Are you here on vacation?" she asked.

"Work. You?"

"Same." Wisteria hesitated, then decided on partial honesty. "I'm a psychologist. I'm here to evaluate someone's... research."

Something flickered in his eyes—interest, wariness, or perhaps recognition. "What kind of research?"

"Medical research. Experimental." She studied his face. "I don't suppose you'd know a Dr. Holdsby Asher?"

The man's expression went very still. For a moment, the only sounds were the jet's engines and the rain hammering against the fuselage. When he spoke, his voice was carefully neutral.

"That's an interesting name. Holdsby. Not very common."

"You know him?"

"I know of him." He was quiet for a moment. "Dr. Vanish, isn't it? Wisteria Vanish?"

Now it was Wisteria's turn to go still. "How do you—"

"I'm Holdsby Asher."

The plane hit another pocket of turbulence, but Wisteria barely noticed. She stared at the man across the aisle—this was the mysterious doctor she'd come to evaluate? He looked nothing like the military photograph Rebecca had shown her. That man had been younger, harder, wearing the confident expression of someone certain of his place in the world. This man carried shadows in his eyes and something indefinable that suggested he'd walked through fire and emerged changed.

"You're not what I expected," she said.

"Neither are you." His dark eyes searched her face. "VitaNuova told you I was dangerous, didn't they? A madman playing with forces beyond his understanding?"

"Something like that."

"And yet you came anyway."

"And yet I came anyway."

The plane touched down with a jarring thud, tires squealing against wet runway. Around them, passengers began gathering their belongings, the usual end-of-flight bustle that felt surreal after their conversation. Wisteria remained frozen in her seat, trying to process this unexpected development.

"Dr. Vanish," Holdsby said quietly, "I should tell you that this meeting isn't a coincidence. I arranged to be on this flight."

"How did you—"

"I have friends in various places. When VitaNuova started making inquiries about psychologists specializing in battlefield trauma, it wasn't hard to narrow down the possibilities. When they settled on you..." He shrugged. "Let's just say I wanted to meet you before you met the official version of me."

"The official version?"

"The version they expect you to see. The mad scientist in his laboratory, playing God with the dead." His smile was bitter. "That version exists, Dr. Vanish. But it's not the whole story."

The plane had come to a complete stop at the gate. Passengers were filing out, their conversations mixing Spanish and English in the easy bilingual flow of regions with a healthy tourism industry. Wisteria realized she was still gripping the chunks of crystallized ginger Holdsby had given her.

"Why did you want to meet me?" she asked.

"Because I know why you're really here. It's not just professional curiosity, is it? VitaNuova found someone who'd lost something they'd do anything to get back."

Wisteria's throat constricted. "You don't know anything about me."

"I know your husband died in Afghanistan. I know you've been barely functioning since. I know you write poetry to try to make sense of a world that took away the person you loved most." His voice was gentle but relentless. "I know because I've been where you are."

"Have you?"

"I lost my entire unit in Fallujah. Twelve men I'd kept alive through two deployments. I couldn't save them when it mattered most." He touched the turquoise bracelet absently. "My grandfather gave me this. Said it would protect me from the spirits of the dead. Turns out he had it backwards."

The last passengers were exiting the plane. A flight attendant approached, smiling professionally.

"Folks, we need to ask you to deplane now."

Holdsby stood and reached for his carry-on bag. "Dr. Vanish—Wisteria—I have a proposition for you."

"I'm listening."

"Don't go to your hotel tonight. Come with me. Let me show you what I've really been doing in Todos Santos. Not the version VitaNuova wants you to see, but the truth."

Wisteria felt as if she were standing at the edge of a cliff, with safety behind her and unknown depths ahead. Everything about this felt dangerous—meeting her subject before the official evaluation, accepting an invitation from a man she'd known for less than an hour, abandoning the careful protocols that had governed her professional life.

But then she thought of David, of the letter she still couldn't bring herself to open, of the empty space in her bed that no amount of therapy or time seemed able to fill.

"One condition," she said, standing and reaching for her own bag. "You tell me why you're really doing this research. Not the scientific justification or the philosophical arguments. The real reason."

Holdsby studied her face for a long moment. Around them, the aircraft was empty except for cleaning crew preparing for the next flight.

"Because the dead don't stay buried, Dr. Vanish. Not when they have unfinished business. And sometimes..." His voice dropped to barely above a whisper. "Sometimes the only way to find peace is to bring them back long enough to say goodbye."

Thunder rumbled outside the aircraft windows. Wisteria looked out at the storm-lashed tarmac of Los Cabos airport, rain streaming down the glass like tears.

"Lead the way, Dr. Asher."

As they walked through the jet bridge into the airport terminal, Wisteria caught her reflection in the window—a blonde woman walking beside a dark-haired man, both of them carrying the particular burden of those who've loved and lost. They looked, she thought, like two people who'd agreed to jump off a cliff together, trusting that they'd figure out how to fly on the way down.

Behind them, the storm continued its assault on the coast of Baja California, as if the sky itself were grieving for all the chances that couldn't be taken back, all the words that couldn't be unsaid, all the dead who couldn't be brought home.

CHAPTER 5: TODOS SANTOS ARRIVAL

The drive from Los Cabos to Todos Santos took them through landscape that seemed to exist in a different century entirely. Holdsby drove a battered Ford pickup, its paint faded by years of desert sun and salt air, while Wisteria sat in the passenger seat watching the Baja California coastline unfold like a fever dream.

To their left, the Pacific Ocean crashed against cliffs carved from ancient volcanic rock, sending spray high enough to catch the last rays of sunset. The water was the color of hammered silver, streaked with foam that glowed phosphorescent in the dying light. To their right, the Sonoran Desert stretched inland, a landscape of impossible geometries—towering cardón cacti that looked like ancient church organs, twisted ocotillo plants reaching toward the sky like the arms of supplicants, and palo verde trees that seemed to glow with their own internal light.

"It's beautiful," Wisteria said, rolling down her window to breathe in air that tasted of salt and sage and something indefinably wild.

"Most people don't see it that way at first," Holdsby replied, navigating around a pothole that could have swallowed a small car. "They see emptiness. Desolation. A place where nothing could possibly live, let alone thrive."

"But you see something else."

"I see a place where life finds a way despite impossible odds. Where things that should be dead somehow keep going." He glanced at her. "It seemed like the right place for my kind of work."

The road curved inland, following arroyos that had been carved by flash floods over millennia. In the distance, mountains rose like the spines of sleeping giants, their peaks still touched with snow despite the desert heat. The geology here told a story of violent upheaval—tectonic plates grinding against each other, volcanoes erupting, ancient seas evaporating to leave behind salt flats that gleamed like mirrors.

"Tell me about Todos Santos," Wisteria said.

"It means 'All Saints.' Founded by Jesuit missionaries in the 18th century as a sugar plantation. The indigenous Pericú people had been living here for thousands of years before that, following the seasonal migrations of whales and sea turtles." Holdsby downshifted as they climbed a hill dotted with elephant trees, their bulbous trunks storing water against the drought that was always coming. "The Spanish brought Christianity and disease in equal measure. By 1840, the Pericú were gone. All dead."

"That's tragic."

"History is full of extinctions, Dr. Vanish. Species, cultures, languages, ways of understanding the world. Sometimes I wonder if that's what I'm really trying to do—prevent another kind of extinction."

They crested the hill, and suddenly Todos Santos spread below them like a village from a different era. Adobe buildings clustered around a central plaza, their walls painted in shades of ochre and turquoise and burnt orange that seemed to capture and hold the last light of day. Palm trees lined streets that followed no particular grid, meandering like dry riverbeds between structures that looked as if they had grown from the earth itself rather than being built upon it.

"Population about 5,000," Holdsby continued as they descended toward the town. "Half locals whose families have been here for generations, half expats who came looking for something they couldn't find in San Francisco or Los Angeles or wherever they fled from. Artists, writers, retired pharmaceutical executives, former aerospace engineers, people who made fortunes in tech and decided they wanted to make art instead."

"And you."

"And me." He smiled, but there was something sad in his expression. "Though I'm not sure what category I fall into."

They drove through the town center, past galleries displaying paintings of desert landscapes and sculptures made from driftwood and rusted metal. A few restaurants were open for dinner, their patios lit by strings of colored bulbs that created pools of warm light in the gathering darkness. Wisteria caught glimpses of people at outdoor tables—couples sharing bottles of wine, families with children running between the tables, groups of friends talking and laughing in the easy way of people who had nowhere else to be.

"It looks peaceful," she said.

"It is, mostly. The kind of place where time moves differently. Where people come to heal, or to hide, or to reinvent themselves entirely." Holdsby turned onto a narrow street lined with bougainvillea that cascaded over adobe walls in waterfalls of purple and red. "I thought it might be a good place to figure out how to live with the dead."

They pulled up in front of a small hotel that looked like it had been transplanted from colonial Mexico—thick walls, heavy wooden doors, a courtyard visible through an arched entrance. A hand-painted sign read "Casa Bentley" in elegant script.

"This is where VitaNuova booked you?" Holdsby asked.

"Yes. Is that a problem?"

"Not a problem. Just... convenient. The owner, Maria Bentley, is... let's say she's sympathetic to unconventional research."

Wisteria studied his face. "You mean she knows what you're doing."

"She knows I'm trying to help people. That's enough for her."

They sat in the truck for a moment, engine ticking as it cooled, while around them Todos Santos settled into evening. Somewhere in the distance, Wisteria could hear music—guitars and voices singing in Spanish, the sound drifting on desert air that carried the scents of blooming jasmine and wood smoke and the faint salt tang of the nearby ocean.

"Dr. Asher—Holdsby—I need to ask you something."

"Go ahead."

"Are you really bringing people back from the dead?"

He was quiet for so long that Wisteria began to think he wouldn't answer. When he finally spoke, his voice was careful, measured.

"Define 'back from the dead,' Dr. Vanish."

"That's not an answer."

"It's the only answer I can give right now. What I'm doing... it's not what you think it is. It's not what VitaNuova thinks it is. It's not even what I thought it was when I started."

"Then what is it?"

Holdsby turned to face her fully, his dark eyes serious. "It's an attempt to understand the space between life and death. The place where consciousness goes when the body fails. And sometimes..." He paused. "Sometimes it's an attempt to reach across that space and bring something back."

"Something?"

"Not someone. Something. Memories. Patterns of thought. Echoes of personality. Whether that constitutes resurrection or just a very sophisticated form of necromancy..." He shrugged. "I suppose that's what you're here to determine."

A woman emerged from the hotel—mid-fifties, silver hair braided down her back, wearing a flowing dress that looked like it had been woven from sunset. She approached the truck with the kind of smile that suggested she'd been expecting them.

"Dr. Vanish?" Her voice carried a slight accent—British, perhaps, or Australian. "I'm Maria Bentley. Welcome to Todos Santos."

Wisteria got out of the truck, accepting Maria's offered hand. The woman's grip was firm, and her eyes held the kind of wisdom that came from years of observing human nature in all its complexity.

"Thank you. This is Dr. Asher."

"Holdsby." Maria's smile widened. "How are the experiments progressing?"

"That's what Dr. Vanish is here to evaluate."

Maria studied Wisteria with frank curiosity. "And what do you think so far?"

"I think," Wisteria said carefully, "that I have a lot more questions than answers."

"Good. That means you're paying attention." Maria gestured toward the hotel entrance. "Your room is ready. Holdsby, will you be joining us for dinner?"

"I should get back to the lab."

"The lab will still be there tomorrow. Tonight, you should eat actual food and have an actual conversation with another human being. Doctor's orders."

Holdsby looked as if he might protest, then seemed to think better of it. "All right. But nothing too elaborate. And no mezcal. Last time you got me drunk, I told you about the time I tried to resurrect my commanding officer's cat."

"Did it work?" Wisteria asked.

"For about six hours. Then it attacked everything that moved and we had to put it down again." Holdsby's expression was perfectly serious. "That's when I realized that bringing something back doesn't always mean bringing it back right."

Maria laughed, a sound like wind chimes in a gentle breeze. "Come inside, both of you. The desert night is beautiful, but it's also full of things that bite."

As they walked through the arched entrance into the hotel courtyard, Wisteria caught a glimpse of her reflection in a darkened window. She looked like someone who'd stepped through a doorway into another world—which, she supposed, was exactly what she'd done.

The courtyard was a small oasis of civilization carved from the desert wilderness. Fountain in the center, bougainvillea climbing the walls, tables set for dinner under strings of lights that cast everything in warm, golden tones. Other guests moved about the space—a couple painting watercolors at a corner table, a man reading a thick novel while sipping wine, a woman practicing guitar in the shadow of a massive fig tree.

"It's lovely," Wisteria said.

"It should be," Maria replied. "I've spent twenty years making it exactly what I wanted—a place where people can disappear for a while and figure out who they're supposed to be."

"Is that what you did?"

"I was a pharmaceutical researcher in London. Made a fortune developing antidepressants, then realized I was more depressed than any of my patients. So I sold everything, bought this place, and started over." Maria settled into a chair at a table set for three. "Best decision I ever made."

Holdsby joined them, having retrieved a bottle of wine from somewhere. "Maria thinks everyone should get a second chance to build their life from scratch."

"Don't you?" Maria asked Wisteria.

Wisteria thought of her life in Norman—the routine of pool, office, home, the careful structure she'd built around her grief like a fortress against the chaos of loss. It had felt safe, predictable, necessary. But sitting here in this desert courtyard, surrounded by people who'd chosen to reinvent themselves entirely, she wondered if safety was just another word for slow death.

"I don't know," she said honestly. "I've spent so much time trying to hold onto the life I had that I've never considered what life I might build instead."

"That's why you're here," Holdsby said quietly. "Not to evaluate my research. To decide whether you want to keep living in the past or start building something new."

As if summoned by their conversation, a server appeared with plates of food—fresh fish grilled with lime and herbs, rice studded with vegetables, tortillas still warm from the comal where they had been cooked. The meal was simple but perfect, each bite carrying the taste of this place where desert met sea, where ancient traditions blended with contemporary dreams.

They ate mostly in comfortable silence, listening to the fountain and the distant sound of waves and the soft conversations of other diners. Wisteria found herself relaxing for the first time in months, the constant tension in her shoulders beginning to ease.

"Tell me about your poetry," Maria said eventually.

Wisteria nearly choked. "How did you—"

"Holdsby mentioned it. I'd love to hear something sometime."

"It's not very good."

"Good is relative. Honest is what matters."

Wisteria glanced at Holdsby, who was studying his plate with apparent fascination. "Most of it is about loss. Grief. The things we can't get back."

"Show me," Maria said.

Before she could lose her nerve, Wisteria pulled out her phone and scrolled to a recent poem. Her voice was barely above a whisper as she read:

"The living build monuments to absence—
Photographs that fade,
Wedding rings that will not budge,
Clothes that still hold
The shape of beloved shoulders.
But the dead build nothing.
They are archaeology,
Waiting to be excavated
By those who loved them
Into meaning."

The courtyard had grown quiet around them. Even the fountain seemed to have hushed its bubbling to listen.

"That's beautiful," Maria said softly. "And heartbreaking."

"It's true," Holdsby added. "The dead don't build anything. We build around them, trying to make sense of their absence."

"Is that what your research is about?" Wisteria asked. "Building something with the dead instead of around them?"

Holdsby met her eyes across the table. "Maybe. Or maybe it's about learning that some kinds of archaeology are too dangerous to attempt."

Later, after Maria had shown Wisteria to her room—a simple space with thick walls that kept out the desert heat and windows that framed views of the courtyard garden—Wisteria stood on her small balcony looking out at the lights of Todos Santos. The town seemed to glow from within, as if each building held secrets that lit up the darkness.

Tomorrow, she would begin her official evaluation of Holdsby's work. Tonight, she was just a woman standing in a desert town at the edge of the known world, wondering if she was brave enough to step across the threshold into whatever came next.

In the distance, coyotes howled at the rising moon, their voices carrying across the desert like prayers offered to gods who might or might not be listening. Wisteria closed her eyes and let the sound wash over her, thinking of all the different ways there were to be alive, and all the different ways there were to be lost.

CHAPTER 6: THE LABORATORY

The abandoned silver mine lay fifteen miles northeast of Todos
Santos, hidden in the Sierra de la Laguna mountains where
ancient granite peaks thrust up from the desert floor like the
vertebrae of some buried giant. Holdsby's truck climbed the
switchback road as the sun reached its zenith, the metal groaning
under the assault of heat that seemed to rise from the earth itself.

Wisteria gripped the door handle as they navigated another
hairpin turn, the Pacific Ocean visible far below them through
gaps in the mountain's spine. The landscape here was
primordial—organ pipe cacti standing sentinel on slopes of
decomposed granite, their green flesh storing decades of precious
water. Brittlebush and ghost plant clung to crevices in the rock,
their silver leaves reflecting light like mirrors to protect against
the killing heat.

"The mine was abandoned in 1958," Holdsby said, downshifting as
they approached a gate that looked like it hadn't been opened in
decades. "Silver played out, and it wasn't economical to go deeper.
The Mexican government was happy to lease it to me for next to
nothing."

He got out to unlock the gate, and Wisteria was struck by the
absolute silence of the place. No birds, no insects, no wind—just
the vast quiet of stone and sky and the weight of geological time.
The gate swung open with a screech that seemed to violate the
sacred stillness.

"How did you find this place?" she asked as they drove through.

"I was looking for somewhere no one would ask questions. Somewhere the dead might feel at home." His smile was grim. "Turned out to be perfect for both requirements."

The mine entrance gaped like a mouth in the mountainside, surrounded by the skeletal remains of ore processing equipment. Rails for mine cars disappeared into darkness that seemed to swallow light itself. But as they drew closer, Wisteria could see that the ruins weren't entirely abandoned—solar panels glinted from concealed positions on the surrounding rocks, and she caught the almost inaudible hum of electrical equipment.

"Most of the lab is underground," Holdsby explained, parking near what looked like a maintenance shed. "Natural climate control, and the mountain blocks most forms of electromagnetic interference. Plus," he added with dark humor, "it feels appropriate."

Inside the shed, a freight elevator descended into the mountain's heart. The walls were carved from living rock, showing the tool marks of miners who'd died decades before Wisteria was born. LED strips provided illumination, but they only emphasized the otherworldly quality of the space—part ancient cave, part high-tech facility.

"How deep are we going?" Wisteria asked.

"About two hundred feet. The lab occupies a natural chamber that the miners expanded. They never knew they'd carved out the perfect place for my kind of research."

The elevator shuddered to a stop, and the doors opened onto a sight that made Wisteria's breath catch. The chamber was enormous—easily the size of a cathedral, with stalactites hanging from the ceiling like stone icicles. But it had been transformed into something between a medical facility and a mad scientist's laboratory.

Banks of computers lined one wall, their screens displaying scrolling data that meant nothing to Wisteria but seemed to pulse with electronic life. Examination tables surrounded by equipment she couldn't identify occupied the center of the space. Glass containers filled with liquids that ranged from clear to deep pink to an unsettling shade of gray covered every available surface.

And in the corners, shadowed but unmistakably present, were tanks filled with floating shapes that might once have been human.

"Welcome to my resurrection chamber," Holdsby said, his voice echoing in the stone space. "Three years of work, twelve million dollars in equipment, and more sleepless nights than I care to count."

Wisteria approached one of the tanks, her psychological training warring with her human revulsion. The shape inside was definitely human—or had been. Male, middle-aged, suspended in fluid that looked like amniotic fluid but smelled of ozone and something organic she couldn't identify.

"Is he...?"

"Dead? Yes. Alive? That's the question you're here to help me answer."

As if summoned by their conversation, the figure in the tank moved. Not much—a slight twitch of the fingers, a barely perceptible shift of the head. But movement nonetheless.

Wisteria stepped back. "How is that possible?"

"The human nervous system doesn't die all at once," Holdsby explained, moving to a computer terminal and calling up displays that showed brainwave patterns, heart rhythms, and other biological data. "Consciousness fades gradually. With the right combination of stem cell therapy, electrical stimulation, and what

I call 'pattern reinforcement,' you can sometimes coax basic functions back online."

"Pattern reinforcement?"

"Memories. Personality traits. The electrical signatures that make someone who they are." He gestured to another bank of equipment. "I record everything during the dying process—brain patterns, neural pathways, the quantum-level activities that might constitute consciousness. Then I try to reintroduce those patterns into the reanimated tissue."

Wisteria felt her worldview tilting on its axis. Everything she'd learned about death, about the finality of loss, about the need to accept and move forward—all of it was being challenged by what she was seeing.

"Does it work?"

"Define 'work.'" Holdsby's voice carried a note of bitter humor. "I can restore basic biological functions about sixty percent of the time. I can occasionally retrieve fragments of memory. But consciousness? Personality? The thing that makes someone who they are rather than just what they are?" He shook his head. "That's proven more elusive."

He led her to another section of the lab where smaller tanks contained what were clearly animal subjects. Dogs, cats, even what looked like a small monkey, all suspended in the same fluid, all showing signs of the same impossible life-in-death.

"I started with animals," Holdsby explained. "Lower cognitive complexity, simpler neural patterns. The results were... mixed."

"Mixed how?"

"See for yourself."

He pressed a series of buttons on a control panel, and one of the tanks began to drain. As the fluid level dropped, the dog inside—a German Shepherd with graying fur—began to show signs of increased animation. Its eyes opened, though they held no recognition, no intelligence. When the tank opened completely, the dog climbed out with movements that were mechanically correct but somehow wrong.

It stood on the lab floor, breathing, alert, but empty. Its eyes were glassy, its movements purposeful but automated. When Holdsby snapped his fingers, the dog turned toward the sound but showed no other response.

"He responds to basic stimuli," Holdsby said. "He'll eat when food is placed in front of him, drink when water is available, even walk when directed. But there's nothing inside. No personality, no learned behaviors, no recognition of his own name. I brought back the machine, but not the ghost."

Wisteria knelt down and extended her hand toward the dog. It looked at her with dead eyes, showing no fear, no curiosity, no emotion of any kind. The sight was profoundly disturbing—life without essence, motion without meaning.

"What happened to him? Before, I mean."

"Hit by a car three days ago. The owner was devastated—a little girl who'd had him since she was five. She begged me to try." Holdsby's voice was heavy with guilt. "I thought if I could perfect the technique on animals first..."

"But you gave her back something that looks like her dog but isn't."

"Yes."

Wisteria stood, backing away from the reanimated animal. "That's monstrous."

"Is it? Or is it hope?" Holdsby's eyes blazed with the passion of someone who'd stared into the abyss and decided to fight back. "Maybe what I'm bringing back isn't the same as what was lost. But it's something. It's not the absolute finality that we're all supposed to accept."

"It's a lie."

"Is comfort always a lie? Is the promise of something better always false?" He gestured around the lab. "Every religion in human history has promised resurrection, life after death, reunion with loved ones. I'm just trying to make good on those promises."

Wisteria thought of David, of the nights she'd lain awake imagining what she'd say to him if she had just five more minutes. Would she care if he came back changed? Would the comfort of his presence be worth the horror of his absence?

"Show me the human subjects," she said.

Holdsby hesitated. "Are you sure? Once you see, you can't unsee."

"I'm here to evaluate your research. I need to see everything."

He led her to the larger tanks where the human subjects floated in their artificial wombs. Up close, the horror was even more pronounced. These had been people—a young woman with tattoos still visible on her arms, an elderly man whose face held the lines of a life fully lived, a teenager whose death must have been sudden and shocking.

"How do you... where do you get them?"

"Terminal patients who volunteer. Accident victims whose families give permission. People who've chosen this instead of traditional burial." Holdsby's voice was defensive. "I don't steal bodies, Dr. Vanish. Everyone here chose to be here."

"And their families? Do they know what they look like now?"

"Some do. Some visit. Others..." He trailed off. "Others find it too difficult."

Wisteria could see why. The figures in the tanks were clearly alive in some biological sense—hearts beating, lungs processing fluid instead of air, basic metabolic functions continuing. But they were also clearly not human in any meaningful sense. They had the same empty quality as the dog, life without soul.

"Have any of them ever shown signs of consciousness? Of being themselves?"

"Fragments. Glimpses. The woman there—Sarah—sometimes moves her lips as if she's trying to speak. The elderly man, Robert, occasionally opens his eyes and looks around with what might be recognition. But it never lasts long, and I can never be sure if it's real consciousness or just random neural firing."

Wisteria approached Sarah's tank, studying the young woman's face. She looked peaceful, almost serene, floating in the pink fluid like some sort of modern Ophelia. But there was something unsettling about the scene that went beyond the obvious wrongness of seeing a dead person alive.

"How long have they been like this?"

"Sarah's been here eight months. Robert, six. The teenager— Michael—just three weeks."

"And they'll stay like this indefinitely?"

"As long as the equipment functions and the nutrient supply continues, yes. They're stable. Not alive in any sense we'd recognize, but not dead either. They exist in a kind of liminal space between states."

Wisteria felt a chill that had nothing to do with the temperature of the underground chamber. "What about decay? Decomposition?"

"The process halts the normal breakdown of tissue. They're essentially preserved at the moment of reanimation. They could theoretically continue like this for decades."

The full horror of what Holdsby was doing began to sink in. He wasn't just bringing people back from the dead—he was trapping them in a state of eternal existence without consciousness, without purpose, without hope. It was a kind of hell disguised as salvation.

"This is wrong," she whispered.

"Is it? Their families have hope. They have the comfort of knowing their loved ones still exist in some form. Isn't that better than the absolute finality of death?"

"It's torture. For them, for their families, for you."

Holdsby's expression hardened. "You haven't lost twelve men who trusted you to keep them alive. You haven't watched people die because you weren't good enough, fast enough, smart enough to save them. This isn't torture, Dr. Vanish. This is penance."

Wisteria realized that she was looking at a man who'd been broken by loss and had channeled that brokenness into something that might be brilliant or might be madness—possibly both. He wasn't a monster, but he was creating monstrous things in his attempt to resurrect not just the dead, but his own sense of purpose and worth.

"What does VitaNuova want with this?" she asked.

"Soldiers who can't die. Warriors who can be killed and brought back to fight again. The ultimate military advantage." His smile was bitter. "They think they can mass-produce resurrection, turn death into a temporary inconvenience."

"Can they?"

"Maybe. Probably. If I can solve the consciousness problem, if I can bring back not just the body but the mind..." He shrugged. "The applications would be limitless. And terrifying."

Wisteria looked around the laboratory one more time—at the banks of computers, the tanks of floating corpses, the equipment that cost more than most people would see in a lifetime. All of it dedicated to the impossible dream of conquering death itself.

"I need some air," she said.

Holdsby nodded. "The surface world does seem simpler after you've spent time down here."

As the elevator carried them back toward sunlight, Wisteria tried to process what she'd seen. Her scientific training told her that Holdsby's research was groundbreaking, potentially revolutionary. Her psychological training suggested he was a traumatized individual working through his grief in the most extreme way possible. Her human heart simply recoiled from the wrongness of it all.

But underneath all of that, in a place she didn't want to acknowledge, a small voice whispered: *What if it worked? What if you could have David back, even changed, even diminished? Wouldn't something be better than nothing?*

The sunlight, when it finally hit her face, felt like absolution. But she knew that the darkness of the mine had already begun to take root inside her, spreading like an infection through everything she thought she knew about life, death, and the terrible space between them.

CHAPTER 7: DESERT NIGHTS

That night, Wisteria couldn't sleep. The thick adobe walls of Casa Bentley that had seemed so comforting the evening before now felt like a tomb, pressing in on her with the weight of what she'd witnessed in Holdsby's laboratory. Every time she closed her eyes, she saw the floating figures in their glass tanks, the empty stare of the reanimated dog, the terrible hope in Holdsby's eyes as he described his work.

At 2 AM, she gave up and wrapped herself in the hotel's cotton robe, stepping out onto her small balcony. The desert night was alive with sounds she was only beginning to recognize—the distant yip of coyotes, the flutter of bats hunting insects, the rustle of creatures moving through the dry brush that surrounded the town. Above, the Milky Way stretched across a sky so clear it seemed like she could reach up and touch the stars.

"Can't sleep either?"

Wisteria turned to find Holdsby sitting on the balcony of the room next to hers, barely visible in the darkness. He was still dressed, as if he'd never even attempted to rest.

"How did you know I was awake?"

"You're not exactly quiet when you're distressed. And after what you saw today..." He shrugged. "I'd be worried if you were sleeping peacefully."

Wisteria pulled her robe tighter against the desert chill. September nights in Baja could be surprisingly cool, the temperature dropping thirty degrees from the day's heat as the thin air released its warmth to the infinite sky.

"Do you ever sleep?"

"Not much. When I do, I dream about the lab. About the people in the tanks. About my unit in Fallujah." His voice was matter-of-fact, as if discussing the weather. "Sleep is overrated when your subconscious is trying to kill you."

"That's not healthy."

"Nothing about my life is healthy, Dr. Vanish. I think we established that today."

A coyote called from somewhere in the hills above town, its voice rising and falling in a haunting melody that spoke of wild places and ancient hungers. Others answered from different directions, their calls weaving together in a chorus that seemed to celebrate the darkness.

"They're beautiful," Wisteria said.

"The locals hate them. They kill chickens, raid garbage cans, occasionally take a small dog or cat. But they were here first. This is their territory, and we're the invaders." Holdsby's voice carried an odd note of admiration. "They adapt, survive, find ways to live with what they've lost. Maybe we could learn something from them."

"Is that what you're doing? Learning to live with loss?"

"I'm learning to fight loss. There's a difference."

Wisteria thought about that distinction as she watched the lights of Todos Santos twinkle below them. Most of the town was asleep, but a few windows glowed with warm light—people reading, working, perhaps dealing with their own sleepless demons.

"Tell me about your unit," she said. "The men you lost."

Holdsby was quiet for so long that she thought he wouldn't answer. When he finally spoke, his voice was barely above a whisper.

"Rodriguez was nineteen. Kid from East LA who joined up to pay for college. Wanted to be a teacher. He carried pictures of his little sister in his helmet—always showing them to anyone who'd look." His laugh was hollow. "Jameson was from Iowa, farm boy who could fix anything with duct tape and determination. Saved our asses more times than I can count with his mechanical skills."

The coyotes had moved closer to town. Wisteria could see their eyes reflecting the scattered streetlights as they moved through the shadows between buildings.

"Thompson was career Army, twenty-year veteran. Should have been safe behind a desk somewhere, but he requested one more deployment. Said his boys needed him." Holdsby's voice cracked slightly. "I couldn't save any of them. Twelve men who trusted me to keep them alive, and I watched every one of them die."

"It wasn't your fault."

"Wasn't it? I was the medic. My job was to keep them breathing long enough to get home to their families. And I failed."

Wisteria heard the sound of liquid being poured and realized Holdsby was drinking something—probably not his first of the night.

"What happened?"

"IED. Buried in the road we'd traveled a dozen times before. Someone had been watching our patrol patterns, learning our routines. The explosion flipped our vehicle, scattered us across fifty meters of desert." His voice took on the clinical tone of someone reciting a medical report. "Rodriguez died instantly— massive head trauma. Jameson bled out before I could get a tourniquet on his leg. Thompson... Thompson took four hours to die. Kept asking for his wife, wanted me to tell her something I couldn't understand because his jaw was shattered."

A bat fluttered past Wisteria's balcony, its erratic flight pattern following insects she couldn't see. Such a small thing, surviving by instinct and adaptation in a harsh environment that offered no guarantees.

"You couldn't have saved them all."

"Maybe not. But I could have saved some of them. If I'd been better trained, better equipped, if I'd made different choices..." He trailed off. "You want to know the worst part? I barely got a scratch. While they were dying around me, I was fine. Explain the justice in that."

"Survivor's guilt is common in—"

"Don't." His voice was sharp. "Don't psychoanalyze me, Dr. Vanish. I know what I am. I'm a man who couldn't do his job when it mattered most, trying to make up for it by doing something that might be impossible."

Wisteria understood, more than she wanted to admit. She'd spent eighteen months trying to find some way to process David's death, some framework that would make sense of a world that had taken him away. The difference was that she'd turned to therapy and poetry and the slow work of healing. Holdsby had turned to resurrection itself.

"What will you do if VitaNuova shuts down your research?"

"They won't. Too much potential, too much military application. They might want to relocate me, bring me back to the States where they can control the work more directly. But they won't shut it down."

"And if they try to?"

"Then I'll disappear. Take the research underground, literally if necessary. There are places in the world where a man with my skills and resources can work without interference."

A night bird called from somewhere in the darkness—not a sound Wisteria recognized, but haunting in its loneliness. She thought of the figures in Holdsby's tanks, suspended between states, neither alive nor dead but something else entirely.

"What about them? The people in your lab?"

"What about them?"

"If you have to run, what happens to them?"

Holdsby was quiet for a moment. "I'd... I'd have to let them go."

"You mean kill them."

"I mean release them from a state they never asked to be trapped in."

The casual way he said it chilled Wisteria more than the desert wind. "You're talking about murder."

"I'm talking about mercy. They're not alive, Dr. Vanish. Not in any meaningful sense. They're biological machines running on autopilot, consciousness trapped in bodies that can't quite die. If I have to choose between preserving their existence and preserving my research..."

"You'd choose the research."

"I'd choose the possibility of perfecting the process. Of maybe bringing someone back whole instead of... whatever they are now."

Wisteria wrapped her robe tighter around herself, but the chill she felt had nothing to do with the temperature. She was sitting next to a man who was capable of killing to protect his work, who saw human lives as acceptable losses in his quest to defeat death itself.

"You scare me," she said quietly.

"I scare myself sometimes." His voice was matter-of-fact. "But fear is just another thing to overcome. Like death, like loss, like the absolute certainty that everything we love will eventually be taken away from us."

"What if acceptance is healthier than fighting? What if some things are meant to be final?"

"Then you're in the wrong place, Dr. Vanish. Because everything I'm doing here is built on the assumption that nothing has to be final. Nothing has to be lost forever."

A coyote appeared in the courtyard below them, moving like liquid shadow between the fountain and the fig tree. It paused to lap at the water, completely unafraid, as if it understood that this was a place where different rules applied.

"Your husband," Holdsby said suddenly. "How did he die?"

The question hit Wisteria like a physical blow. "IED. Outside Kandahar."

"Same as Rodriguez, then. Quick, or did he suffer?"

"I don't know. They wouldn't tell me details."

"That means he suffered. If it had been quick, they would have said so. It's the details they withhold that tell you everything you need to know."

Wisteria felt tears starting to form. "Why are you telling me this?"

"Because you need to understand what you're really choosing between. The comfort of uncertainty versus the horror of knowledge. The peace of letting go versus the torment of holding on." His voice was gentle now, almost hypnotic. "I could bring him back, you know. If you had tissue samples, personal items that carried his genetic signature... the process works better with fresher material, but it's not impossible."

"Stop."

"Think about it. One more conversation. A chance to say goodbye properly. To tell him the things you never got to say."

"I said stop."

But Holdsby continued, relentless. "Even if he came back changed, diminished, wouldn't it be worth it? Wouldn't something be better than nothing?"

Wisteria stood abruptly, her chair scraping against the balcony's tile floor. "I'm going inside."

"Sleep well, Dr. Vanish. But think about what I said. Because tomorrow, I'm going to show you something that might change everything you believe about the finality of death."

Wisteria fled to her room, slamming the balcony door behind her. But even as she pulled the curtains shut and burrowed under the covers, she could hear the coyotes calling to each other in the darkness, their voices speaking of hunger and loss and the endless struggle to survive in a world that offered no guarantees.

And somewhere underneath their wild song, she could hear Holdsby's words echoing in her mind: *Wouldn't something be better than nothing?*

She lay awake until dawn, wrestling with a question that had no good answer, while outside the desert night slowly gave way to another day in a place where the impossible had become routine and death was just another problem to be solved.

CHAPTER 8: THE EXTORTIONIST'S WEB

Jackson Reeves arrived in Todos Santos like a gray cloud drifting across a perfect sky—unremarkable until you noticed how everything around him seemed to dim. He checked into the Hotel California on the opposite side of town from Casa Bentley, a deliberate choice that allowed him to observe without being observed. His room overlooked the main plaza, giving him sight lines to most of the town's commercial district and several of its primary access roads.

From his window, he could see the morning rhythm of the town— local women walking to market with woven baskets, children in school uniforms chattering as they navigated the narrow streets, tourists beginning their daily pilgrimage to galleries and cafes. It was the kind of place that marketed itself as authentic Mexico, unspoiled by the commercialism of Cabo San Lucas, but Reeves knew better. Every place had its price, every person their leverage point. You just had to know where to look.

He set up his equipment with the methodical precision of someone who'd done this hundreds of times before. Telephoto lenses, digital recording devices, satellite communication gear that could reach VitaNuova's headquarters in Virginia instantly. Most importantly, he unpacked his collection of fountain pens—vintage Montblancs and Pelikans that wrote with the kind of authority that modern technology couldn't replicate.

Handwritten notes carried weight that emails never could. There was something about seeing your name inscribed in permanent ink that made even the most hardened individuals reconsider their choices.

His first target was Maria Bentley.

Reeves had done his research during the flight from Los Angeles. Maria had been Dr. Maria Thornfield before she'd disappeared to Mexico, a pharmaceutical researcher whose antidepressant patents had made her wealthy enough to buy a small hotel and retire at fifty. But wealth hadn't protected her from scandal—her research had been compromised by falsified data, and she'd fled the UK just ahead of criminal charges.

Everyone, Reeves reflected as he selected a 1952 Montblanc 149, had something to hide.

The note was brief, written in his careful copperplate script:

Dr. Thornfield,

We should discuss your guests and their research. The UK's statute of limitations on scientific fraud is longer than you might remember.

Room 23, Hotel California. This evening at sunset.

A friend

He sealed it in an envelope and walked to Casa Bentley, timing his arrival for the mid-morning lull when most guests would be exploring the town. The desk clerk, a young man barely out of his teens, accepted the envelope without question when Reeves explained it was a dinner invitation for Señora Bentley.

"Shall I give it to her now?" the clerk asked.

"This evening would be better. After six, if you please."

Reeves left a fifty-dollar tip—enough to ensure compliance without raising suspicion—and walked back toward the plaza. He had other preparations to make.

Dr. Wisteria Vanish was proving more interesting than VitaNuova's files had suggested. Their background check had painted her as a grieving widow whose judgment might be compromised by emotional trauma—easy to manipulate, easier to control. But watching her through telephoto lenses as she moved through town, Reeves saw someone more resilient than expected.

She walked like an athlete, with the confident stride of someone accustomed to physical challenges. Her interactions with locals showed cultural sensitivity and genuine curiosity rather than tourist condescension. Most telling, she'd spent considerable time sitting alone in the plaza, writing in what appeared to be a journal—not the behavior of someone who'd lost herself to grief.

VitaNuova might have underestimated Dr. Vanish. Reeves made a mental note to adjust his approach accordingly.

Holdsby Asher was a different problem entirely.

Reeves had worked with damaged veterans before, understood the particular combination of skills and instabilities that military trauma could produce. Asher was dangerous not because he was unstable—quite the opposite. He was dangerous because he'd found a purpose that gave structure to his damage, channeling his guilt and rage into something that might actually work.

The preliminary reports from VitaNuova's technical assessment team were troubling. Asher's research showed genuine promise, his methods were scientifically sound, and his results—while limited—suggested possibilities that could revolutionize modern warfare. But he was also clearly uncontrollable, operating outside any ethical framework, pursuing goals that extended far beyond mere scientific discovery.

Men like Asher didn't respond to traditional pressure. They'd already lost everything that mattered to them, which made them nearly impossible to threaten or bribe. But they could be redirected, their obsessions channeled toward more useful ends.

Reeves spent the afternoon establishing his surveillance network. Todos Santos was small enough that three well-placed observation points could monitor most of the town's activity. He rented a second-floor apartment overlooking the road to Asher's laboratory, installed cameras with motion sensors and long-range wireless transmitters. A local teenager, eager to earn American dollars, agreed to monitor the equipment in exchange for more money than he'd see in six months of normal work.

By evening, Reeves had a complete picture of Asher's daily routine, Vanish's movement patterns, and the social dynamics of the expatriate community that might be exploited if pressure needed to be applied.

Maria Bentley arrived at sunset, as requested.

She knocked on his door with the confident rap of someone who'd decided not to be intimidated, then entered when he called for her to come in. She was smaller than he'd expected, but there was steel in her gray eyes and a set to her shoulders that suggested she wouldn't be easily broken.

"Dr. Thornfield," Reeves said, not rising from his chair by the window. "Thank you for coming."

"It's Bentley now. Has been for twenty years."

"Of course. Please, sit."

She remained standing. "What do you want?"

"Direct. I appreciate that." Reeves gestured toward a second chair. "I represent certain interests that are concerned about the research being conducted by your guest, Dr. Asher."

"What sort of interests?"

"The sort that prefer their investments to remain stable and their researchers to remain... cooperative."

Maria's expression didn't change, but Reeves caught the slight tension in her shoulders. "Holdsby isn't my responsibility. He's a paying guest, nothing more."

"Who happens to be conducting illegal medical experiments in an abandoned mine. Who happens to be harboring stolen biological material. Who happens to be violating approximately seventeen different international treaties regarding human experimentation."

"I wouldn't know anything about that."

Reeves selected another fountain pen—a Pelikan 400 with green stripes—and began writing on hotel stationary. "Dr. Maria Thornfield, wanted by Interpol for scientific fraud, money laundering, and conspiracy to distribute controlled substances. Current location: Todos Santos, Mexico, operating under false identity."

He looked up at her. "Shall I continue?"

Maria sat down.

"Better." Reeves capped the pen and set it aside. "I'm not here to threaten you, Dr. Bentley. I'm here to offer you an opportunity to be helpful."

"Helpful how?"

"Dr. Vanish is evaluating Dr. Asher's research on behalf of my employers. We want to ensure she has access to all relevant information—including information that Dr. Asher might prefer to keep private."

"You want me to spy on my guests."

"I want you to facilitate communication. Dr. Vanish is a scientist, after all. Scientists appreciate data, documentation, evidence of claims made by their subjects."

Reeves opened his briefcase and withdrew a thick manila folder. "These are photographs from Dr. Asher's laboratory, taken by our technical team during their preliminary assessment. Images that Dr. Vanish might find... illuminating."

Maria glanced at the folder but didn't reach for it. "What's in there?"

"Evidence that Dr. Asher's research extends considerably beyond what he's shown Dr. Vanish. Evidence of human test subjects who weren't volunteers. Evidence of procedures that would constitute torture under any reasonable definition."

"That's impossible. Holdsby would never—"

"Dr. Asher is a man driven by guilt and obsession, operating without oversight in a foreign country where he can purchase silence as easily as laboratory equipment. What did you think would happen?"

Reeves could see Maria processing this, her scientific training warring with her personal loyalty to someone she clearly considered a friend.

"Even if that were true," she said finally, "why would you want Dr. Vanish to know? Wouldn't that compromise your investment?"

"On the contrary. My employers need to understand exactly what they're investing in. If Dr. Asher's methods are effective but unethical, they need to know so they can provide proper oversight. If his methods are both effective and replicable, they need to know so they can begin scaling up production."

"And if his methods don't work?"

"Then they need to know so they can terminate their investment and pursue other avenues."

Reeves stood and walked to the window, watching the last light fade from the plaza below. Tourists were beginning to emerge for dinner, their voices mixing with the sound of guitar music from the restaurant patios.

"Dr. Bentley, you're a scientist. You understand that research without oversight leads to catastrophe. Dr. Asher is brilliant, but he's also unstable. Left to his own devices, he'll either produce something revolutionary or something monstrous. Possibly both."

"So you want to control him."

"I want to protect him. From himself, from his obsessions, from the consequences of unchecked experimentation." Reeves turned back to face her. "And I want to protect Dr. Vanish from making recommendations based on incomplete information."

Maria was quiet for a long moment, studying the folder on the table between them. "What exactly are you asking me to do?"

"Simply ensure that Dr. Vanish sees these photographs. How you accomplish that is entirely up to you."

"And if I refuse?"

"Then tomorrow morning, the Mexican authorities will receive an anonymous tip about a British fugitive operating a hotel in Todos Santos under false documentation."

Maria's smile was bitter. "So much for not threatening me."

"I prefer to think of it as clarifying your options." Reeves returned to his chair, his voice remaining conversational. "You're a pragmatic woman, Dr. Bentley. You've survived in Mexico for twenty years by understanding when to compromise and when to resist. This is clearly a time for compromise."

Maria reached for the folder, her fingers hesitating just above its surface. "How do I know these photographs are real? That you haven't fabricated evidence to serve your purposes?"

"You don't. But you're welcome to verify them. Ask Dr. Asher direct questions about his research methods. Visit the laboratory yourself if he'll permit it. I suspect you'll find that the truth is even more disturbing than what's documented in those images."

The folder felt heavier than it should have when Maria finally picked it up. She didn't open it immediately, instead holding it like something that might explode.

"There's something else you should know," Reeves continued. "Dr. Vanish isn't just here as an evaluator. She's here because she lost her husband in Afghanistan, and she's desperate enough to believe that Dr. Asher might be able to bring him back."

"That's ridiculous. Holdsby's work doesn't—"

"Doesn't it? How do you know what Dr. Asher has told her in private? How do you know what promises he's made, what hopes he's encouraged?" Reeves leaned forward. "A grieving widow with a background in trauma psychology, offered the possibility of resurrection by a charismatic researcher with unlimited funding and no oversight. What could possibly go wrong?"

Maria opened the folder.

The first photograph showed a section of Asher's laboratory that Wisteria hadn't seen—a room filled with smaller tanks containing what appeared to be human organs floating in preservative fluid. Hearts, lungs, brains, all connected to monitoring equipment that tracked their biological functions.

The second photograph showed surgical procedures being performed on clearly deceased subjects—incisions, implantations, modifications that would have been illegal in any legitimate medical facility.

The third photograph was the worst. It showed Asher himself, dressed in surgical scrubs, standing over a table where something that had once been human was connected to dozens of cables and tubes. The figure on the table was moving, its mouth open in what might have been a scream, while Asher made notes on a clipboard.

"Dear God," Maria whispered.

"There are seventeen more photographs," Reeves said quietly. "Each one more disturbing than the last. This is what Dr. Asher calls research. This is what VitaNuova is funding."

Maria closed the folder, her face pale. "How long has this been going on?"

"Our surveillance suggests approximately six months. The subjects appear to be local residents who disappeared without explanation—homeless individuals, undocumented workers, people whose absence wouldn't be immediately noticed."

"I don't believe it. Holdsby wouldn't... he's trying to help people, trying to heal—"

"He's trying to perfect a process that he's convinced himself justifies any means necessary. The difference between healing and torment is often just a matter of perspective, Dr. Bentley."

Reeves stood again, walking to his briefcase and withdrawing a second, smaller envelope. "This contains detailed instructions for ensuring Dr. Vanish sees these photographs in a way that appears natural. You'll also find contact information for reporting back to me about her reactions and any decisions she makes regarding her evaluation."

"You want me to spy on her too."

"I want you to protect her. From Dr. Asher, from her own desperation, from making choices that she'll regret for the rest of her life." His voice carried a note of what might have been genuine concern. "Dr. Vanish is a good person caught in an impossible situation. She deserves to make her decisions based on complete information."

Maria took the second envelope with obvious reluctance. "And what if she decides to expose everything? What if she reports Holdsby to the authorities?"

"Then she'll be making an informed decision based on accurate information. Which is all anyone can ask for."

"But that's not what VitaNuova wants."

"VitaNuova wants Dr. Asher's research. If it's viable, they'll find ways to continue it under proper oversight. If it's not viable, they'll cut their losses and move on to other projects. Either way, they need accurate assessment, not wishful thinking based on incomplete data."

Reeves walked Maria to the door, his manner remaining cordial despite the coercion that had brought her there. "I appreciate your cooperation, Dr. Bentley. And I want you to know that your past... indiscretions... need never become public knowledge if you handle this situation appropriately."

"You mean if I betray my friend."

"I mean if you help prevent a tragedy that's already in motion. Dr. Asher is brilliant, but he's also dangerous. Left unchecked, he'll destroy himself and everyone around him. You have the opportunity to prevent that outcome."

After Maria left, Reeves returned to his window overlooking the plaza. The evening crowd was in full swing now—families strolling between restaurants, street musicians setting up for the night's performances, vendors hawking handmade crafts to tourists eager for authentic Mexican experiences.

None of them knew that their peaceful little town was harboring research that violated every ethical principle of modern medicine. None of them suspected that the charming doctor who occasionally appeared in their cafes and markets was conducting experiments that would have made Dr. Mengele proud.

But that would change soon enough.

Reeves opened his laptop and began typing his evening report to VitaNuova headquarters. The operation was proceeding according to plan. Dr. Vanish would soon have access to information that would force her to confront the true nature of Dr. Asher's work. Her reaction to that information would determine VitaNuova's next steps.

If she remained committed to protecting Asher despite evidence of his crimes, she would become a liability to be managed.

If she attempted to expose the research publicly, she would become a threat to be neutralized.

If she agreed to help VitaNuova gain control over Asher's methods while ensuring proper oversight, she would become a valuable asset.

The beauty of the situation was that Reeves was prepared for all three possibilities.

He finished his report and selected another fountain pen—a vintage Waterman with a gold nib that wrote like silk on paper. The note he composed was brief but carefully crafted:

Dr. Vanish,

Tomorrow you will learn things about Dr. Asher's research that will challenge everything you believe about his work. When that moment comes, remember that some choices cannot be undone, and some knowledge cannot be unknown.

Choose wisely.

A concerned observer

He sealed the note in an envelope and set it aside for morning delivery. Then he poured himself three fingers of scotch from the bottle he'd brought from Los Angeles and settled in to watch the night descend on Todos Santos.

Somewhere in the hills above town, Dr. Asher was probably working in his underground laboratory, pursuing his obsession with the same single-minded determination that had made him an effective combat medic and now made him a dangerous researcher.

Somewhere in Casa Bentley, Dr. Vanish was probably struggling with what she'd seen, trying to reconcile the horror of Asher's methods with the hope his results might represent.

And somewhere between them, Maria Bentley was probably staring at a folder full of photographs that would change everything, wondering how she'd become complicit in something she didn't fully understand.

Reeves sipped his scotch and smiled. He'd spent thirty years managing situations like this—complex operations where multiple parties had conflicting interests and incomplete information. The key was patience, precision, and the understanding that everyone, eventually, could be motivated to serve someone else's purposes.

Even the righteous. Even the desperate. Even the brilliant.

Especially the brilliant.

Tomorrow would bring revelations that would reshape the entire operation. Dr. Vanish would be forced to confront truths that would test every principle she held dear. Dr. Asher would discover that his secret research wasn't as secret as he'd believed. And VitaNuova would move one step closer to acquiring technology that could revolutionize modern warfare.

Or destroy it entirely.

Either outcome was acceptable to Jackson Reeves. In his experience, chaos was just another word for opportunity, and opportunity was what separated the successful from the merely competent.

He raised his glass to the window, toasting the lights of Todos Santos and the complex web of manipulation he'd woven around its unwitting residents.

"To new beginnings," he murmured, and drank deeply.

Outside, the desert night settled over the town like a blanket, hiding secrets that tomorrow would bring screaming into the light.

CHAPTER 9: EL PROSTÍBULO

The photographs arrived with Wisteria's morning coffee, slipped under her door sometime before dawn by hands that left no trace. She found them when she stepped onto her balcony to watch the sunrise paint the Sierra de la Laguna mountains in shades of gold and crimson—seventeen images that shattered her understanding of everything she'd seen in Holdsby's laboratory.

The first showed surgical procedures being performed on conscious subjects, their eyes wide with terror above restraints that held them motionless. The second revealed chambers she hadn't been shown, filled with partially dissected corpses connected to machines that kept isolated organs functioning. The third depicted Holdsby himself, clinical and detached, making notes while something that might once have been human writhed on an examination table.

Wisteria sat heavily in her balcony chair, the photographs scattered across the small table like evidence of crimes against reality itself. Each image challenged not just her assessment of Holdsby's research, but her fundamental assumptions about the nature of consciousness, suffering, and what it meant to be human.

If consciousness is constructed through social interaction, she thought, remembering her graduate seminars on Peter Berger and Thomas Luckmann, *what happens when that construction breaks down? When the boundary between self and other, between life and death, becomes negotiable?*

She thought of Sartre's concept of radical freedom—the terrible responsibility that came with the knowledge that existence precedes essence, that humans must create meaning in a universe that provided none inherently. Holdsby had taken that freedom to its logical extreme, deciding that death itself was just another social construct to be deconstructed and rebuilt according to his own design.

But whose meaning was being created in that underground laboratory? Whose reality was being constructed?

A knock at her door interrupted her philosophical spiral. Maria Bentley stood in the hallway, her face pale and drawn, holding a manila envelope that Wisteria recognized as the source of the photographs.

"We need to talk," Maria said.

They sat in the hotel's courtyard, the morning bustle of Todos Santos providing a surreal backdrop to their conversation. Children walked to school past the fountain where Maria had served dinner just days before, their laughter mixing with the sound of water over stone while the two women discussed evidence of horrors that violated every principle of medical ethics.

"How long have you known?" Wisteria asked.

"I didn't. Not until last night." Maria's hands trembled as she poured coffee from a ceramic pot. "Someone came to see me. Someone who knew about my past, about why I really left England."

"Who?"

"He called himself a concerned observer. Professional, well-dressed, the kind of man who makes threats sound like helpful suggestions." Maria's laugh was bitter. "He wanted me to ensure you saw these photographs. Said you deserved to make your evaluation based on complete information."

Wisteria studied the older woman's face, noting the shadows under her eyes, the way her shoulders curved inward as if protecting herself from invisible blows. "What did he threaten you with?"

"Exposure. Deportation. Prison." Maria shrugged. "The usual consequences of running away from your mistakes instead of facing them."

The philosophical implications struck Wisteria with unexpected force. Here was the social construction of reality in its rawest form—a woman who'd spent twenty years building a new identity in a foreign country, only to discover that her constructed self was as fragile as tissue paper when confronted with determined opposition.

"But that's not why I'm showing you this," Maria continued. "I'm showing you because I think you're in danger. Not just from Holdsby, but from yourself. From the part of you that's desperate enough to believe that any price is worth paying for another chance."

Wisteria thought of Kierkegaard's leap of faith, the existential moment when reason fails and one must choose to believe or despair. "What if the price is worth paying? What if bringing someone back, even diminished, even changed, is better than accepting their permanent absence?"

"Look at the photographs again," Maria said quietly. "Really look at them. Those people in Holdsby's laboratory—they're not diminished or changed. They're tortured. They're trapped in a state that's neither life nor death, consciousness without agency, existence without meaning."

Wisteria looked again, forcing herself to see past her own desperate hope to the reality documented in the images. The subjects weren't just reanimated—they were aware enough to suffer, conscious enough to experience terror, but powerless to communicate or escape their condition.

"He's not bringing people back," she realized. "He's creating a new form of hell."

"And he's convinced himself it's research. That the suffering is temporary, that perfecting the process will somehow justify the means." Maria leaned forward. "That's how atrocities happen, Dr. Vanish. Good people convince themselves that their noble ends justify terrible means, and before they know it, they've become the monsters they thought they were fighting."

The weight of existential responsibility settled over Wisteria like a physical presence. Sartre had written that we are "condemned to be free"—that every choice we make defines not just ourselves, but our understanding of what humanity should be. Her evaluation of Holdsby's research wasn't just a professional assessment; it was a statement about the kind of reality she was willing to help construct.

"Where is he getting the subjects?" she asked.

"I don't know. But I suspect..." Maria hesitated. "There's a place in Cabo San Lucas. A brothel that caters to very specific clientele. Young women who've disappeared from other places, who have no families to report them missing, no legal status to protect them."

The euphemism hit Wisteria like a physical blow. Sex trafficking. Women reduced to commodities, their personhood already stripped away by social systems that treated them as disposable. Perfect subjects for someone who needed test material that wouldn't be missed.

"He's experimenting on trafficking victims?"

"I don't know for certain. But the logic is... appalling in its efficiency. Women who are already socially invisible, already existing outside normal legal protections, already treated as objects rather than people."

Wisteria felt nauseous. The philosophical abstractions she'd been wrestling with suddenly became concrete, personal, unbearably real. This wasn't about the nature of consciousness or the social construction of death—this was about power, exploitation, and the reduction of human beings to raw material for someone else's obsession.

"I have to see for myself," she said.

"What?"

"The brothel. I have to know if that's where he's getting his subjects."

Maria stared at her. "That's incredibly dangerous. These aren't people who respond well to curiosity."

"Then what do you suggest? That I complete my evaluation based on incomplete information? That I recommend VitaNuova continue funding research that might be built on human trafficking?"

The older woman was quiet for a long moment, watching the fountain cycle water through its ancient patterns. "There's something else you should consider," she said finally. "The possibility that you're not here to evaluate Holdsby's research at all."

"What do you mean?"

"Think about it. VitaNuova could have sent a team of scientists, military researchers, people with direct expertise in biomedical technology. Instead, they sent a trauma psychologist whose husband died in Afghanistan. Someone whose judgment might be compromised by personal loss."

The implication hung between them like smoke from a distant fire. "You think this is a setup?"

"I think you're being manipulated. By VitaNuova, by Holdsby, possibly by both. The question is whether you're being manipulated into supporting his research or destroying it."

Wisteria considered this from an existentialist perspective. If her freedom to choose was being constrained by forces she didn't understand, if her reality was being constructed by others for their own purposes, then her first responsibility was to reclaim her agency—to act authentically rather than reactively.

"Then I need more information," she said. "About the brothel, about VitaNuova's real intentions, about what Holdsby is actually doing with his research."

"And how exactly do you propose to get that information?"

Wisteria thought of Sartre's concept of "bad faith"—the tendency to deny one's freedom and responsibility by pretending to be constrained by external forces. She'd been operating in bad faith since David's death, allowing her grief to define her choices, accepting the role of victim rather than claiming the power to act.

"By going to Cabo San Lucas. By visiting this brothel and seeing what's really happening there."

"That's insane."

"Maybe. But staying here and pretending I can make an ethical evaluation without understanding the full scope of what I'm evaluating—that's not just insane, it's cowardly."

Maria studied her face for a long moment. "You're not just talking about the research anymore, are you? You're talking about your husband, about whether bringing him back would be worth it regardless of the cost to others."

The observation cut deeper than Wisteria had expected. She'd been thinking of David constantly since arriving in Todos Santos, imagining conversations they might have, words she might finally be able to say. But she'd also been thinking of the women in those photographs, reduced to test subjects for someone else's grief.

"I'm talking about taking responsibility for my choices," she said. "About refusing to let other people construct my reality for me."

"Even if it means discovering things you'd rather not know?"

"Especially then."

That afternoon, Wisteria rented a car and drove toward Cabo San Lucas, leaving Todos Santos by the coastal highway that curved through landscape that seemed designed to induce philosophical contemplation. To her left, the Pacific Ocean stretched to a horizon that blurred the distinction between water and sky. To her right, desert mountains rose in geological layers that told stories of deep time, of forces so vast and slow that human concerns seemed momentarily irrelevant.

But human concerns had a way of reasserting themselves, especially when those concerns involved suffering on a scale that challenged one's faith in the possibility of meaning.

The brothel was located in a part of Cabo San Lucas that tourists never saw—a collection of concrete buildings behind a chain-link fence, unmarked except for a small sign in Spanish that advertised "Private Massage Services." The area smelled of industrial disinfectant and something organic that might have been fear.

Wisteria parked across the street and observed the facility through telephoto lenses she'd borrowed from a photographer staying at Casa Bentley. The comings and goings followed a predictable pattern—men arriving alone in expensive cars, staying for predetermined periods, leaving without looking back.

86

Security was minimal but professional, suggesting an operation that relied more on discretion than force.

But it was the women she glimpsed through windows that confirmed her worst suspicions. Young, obviously foreign, with the hollow-eyed look of people who'd had their agency systematically stripped away. They moved with the mechanical precision of the reanimated subjects in Holdsby's laboratory—alive but not living, conscious but not free.

The social construction of reality, Wisteria thought grimly, *includes the construction of some people as less real than others.*

As she watched, a familiar truck pulled up to the facility's side entrance. Holdsby Asher emerged, carrying a medical bag and moving with the confident stride of someone who belonged there. He disappeared through a door marked "Private," and Wisteria realized she was witnessing the recruitment process firsthand.

He wasn't just experimenting on trafficking victims. He was participating in their trafficking, using his medical credentials to evaluate potential subjects, selecting those who met his research criteria.

The philosophical implications hit her like a physical blow. This wasn't just about the nature of consciousness or the ethics of resurrection—this was about the systematic dehumanization of vulnerable people, the reduction of complex human beings to raw material for someone else's obsession with conquering death.

Zombie prostitutes. Was it better to reanimate a person from the dead to perform sex work, or was it better to kidnap and trick young women into human trafficking? And, was it better for a customer to have relations with someone it could not actually hurt any more? (at least as far as one might imagine.)

Nightmare beyond nightmare.

Sartre had written about the "look" of the other—the moment when one recognizes another person as equally real, equally deserving of moral consideration. Holdsby had systematically trained himself not to see that look, to view these women as objects rather than subjects, materials rather than people.

But Wisteria saw it. In the brief glimpses she caught through windows, in the way the women moved and carried themselves, in the terrible awareness that flickered behind their eyes despite their circumstances. They were as real as she was, as deserving of life and freedom and the chance to construct their own meaning.

As the sun set over Cabo San Lucas, painting the sky in shades that would have been beautiful under other circumstances, Wisteria sat in her rental car and tried to process what she'd witnessed. The research she'd come to evaluate wasn't just unethical—it was built on a foundation of human trafficking, sexual exploitation, and the systematic denial of personhood to vulnerable women.

And she was complicit in it simply by being there, by accepting VitaNuova's funding, by allowing herself to be positioned as an "objective" evaluator of research that was fundamentally subjective in its cruelty.

Her phone buzzed. A text from an unknown number: *Did you find what you were looking for?*

Another message followed: *Some knowledge changes you. The question is whether you'll use that change to serve truth or comfort.*

A third: *Choose carefully, Dr. Vanish. Some choices echo across more lives than just your own.*

Wisteria turned off her phone and started the car. The drive back to Todos Santos would give her time to think, to process what she'd seen, to decide what kind of reality she was willing to help construct.

But already, she knew that her evaluation of Holdsby's research had fundamentally changed. This wasn't about the possibility of resurrection anymore. It was about the responsibility that came with knowledge, and the terrible freedom to choose between truth and complicity.

The desert highway stretched before her like a philosophical argument made manifest—empty, demanding, offering no easy answers to questions that seemed to grow more complex with every mile.

CHAPTER 10: HEART OF A DOG

That night, Holdsby found Wisteria sitting by the fountain in Casa Bentley's courtyard, staring into water that reflected stars she couldn't name. The hotel's other guests had retired hours ago, leaving them alone with the sound of moving water and the distant cries of night birds hunting in the desert beyond the town's edges.

"You went to Cabo San Lucas today," he said, settling into the chair across from her without invitation.

"How did you know?"

"Maria told me. She's worried about you." His dark eyes studied her face in the fountain's reflected light. "She thinks you're losing perspective, allowing emotional involvement to compromise your professional judgment."

Wisteria laughed, but there was no humor in it. "Professional judgment. As if there's anything professional about what you're doing."

"What I'm doing is pushing the boundaries of human knowledge. Exploring possibilities that conventional ethics have declared off-limits." Holdsby's voice carried the calm certainty of someone who'd rehearsed these justifications countless times. "Every significant advance in medical science has required researchers willing to challenge existing moral frameworks."

"Is that how you justify using trafficking victims as test subjects?"

The accusation hung between them like smoke from a distant fire. Holdsby's expression didn't change, but something shifted behind his eyes—a calculation being performed, options being weighed.

"You saw the facility," he said finally.

"I saw you entering it with a medical bag. I saw you participating in their operation."

"And what did you conclude from that observation?"

Wisteria thought of Sartre's writings on "bad faith"—the tendency to deny one's freedom and responsibility by pretending to be constrained by circumstances beyond one's control. "I concluded that you've convinced yourself that the ends justify the means, regardless of how those means involve the dehumanization of vulnerable people."

"Dehumanization." Holdsby tasted the word as if it were wine. "That's an interesting concept. What makes someone human, Dr. Vanish? Consciousness? The ability to suffer? Social recognition? Legal status?"

"The inherent dignity that comes with being a sentient being capable of experiencing both pain and meaning."

"And if that dignity has already been stripped away by social systems that treat certain people as disposable? If society has already decided that some lives matter less than others?" His voice remained calm, philosophical. "Am I creating victims, or am I simply working with victims that society has already created?"

The question forced Wisteria to confront uncomfortable truths about the social construction of worth, about how societies determine which lives have value and which can be sacrificed for the greater good. But recognizing the existence of systematic dehumanization didn't justify participating in it.

"You're making it worse," she said. "You're taking people who've already been victimized and subjecting them to additional suffering."

"Am I? Or am I offering them something that society never would—the possibility of transcending the limitations that biology and circumstance have imposed on them?"

Holdsby stood and walked to the fountain, trailing his fingers in water that caught starlight like liquid diamonds. "The women you saw today—they're going to die, Dr. Vanish. Maybe from disease, maybe from violence, maybe from the simple grinding poverty that makes their lives unsustainable. Society has already written them off as acceptable losses."

"So you're saving them?"

"I'm offering them immortality. Consciousness unbound by the limitations of a single, fragile body. The chance to exist beyond the social constraints that have defined their worth since birth."

Immortality to do what?? Wisteria's first response was outrage. Resurrect a German Shepherd so he could continue to make his owner feel happy? Did the dog suffer the pains of its mortal injuries, or were they miraculously healed?

And, well, for the trafficked women, Wisteria had no words. Historically, women were always "trafficked" – whether for the furtherance of family wealth, as in the case of women in Jane Austen's times, or for building riches for transnational criminal organizations and their evil politician enablers.

The philosophical implications of the argument he was making of "offering immortality" were as seductive as they were horrifying. If individual identity was indeed socially constructed, if personhood was something granted or withheld by cultural consensus, then perhaps traditional concepts of dignity and autonomy were themselves tools of oppression.

But Wisteria had seen the terror in the eyes of his test subjects, had witnessed the suffering of beings who retained enough consciousness to experience pain but lacked the agency to escape it.

"What you're creating isn't transcendence," she said. "It's a new form of slavery. Consciousness without freedom, existence without purpose."

"Because I haven't perfected the process yet. But every iteration brings me closer to success, to the possibility of resurrection that preserves not just biological function but complete psychological continuity."

"And how many people suffer for your learning curve?"

Holdsby turned to face her, his expression serious but unrepentant. "How many people suffered for every medical advance in human history? I would argue that they were suffering anyway. At least, there's some sort of option."

Wisteria maintained silence. She wondered where he would go with this. How far would he take it?

"How many soldiers have died for every war that preserved the values you claim to defend? The question isn't whether people die—they're dying anyway. The question is whether their deaths serve a purpose larger than themselves."

Wisteria thought of Camus's writings on the absurd—the conflict between human need for meaning and the universe's apparent indifference to that need. Holdsby had resolved that conflict by deciding that he could create meaning through force of will, that his desire to conquer death was sufficient justification for any action.

But Camus had also written about rebellion—the need to act authentically in the face of absurdity, to create value through solidarity with other conscious beings rather than through domination over them.

"Show me," she said.

"Show you what?"

"Your latest experiment. The one that's closest to success. I want to see what you consider progress."

Holdsby studied her face for a long moment. "Are you sure? Once you see, you become complicit. Your knowledge makes you responsible for whatever happens next."

"I'm already complicit. I've been complicit since I accepted VitaNuova's money and agreed to evaluate research I didn't fully understand."

"Very well. But remember—you asked for this."

They drove through the desert night back toward the abandoned mine, the truck's headlights carving tunnels of visibility through darkness that seemed to swallow light itself. The silence between them was heavy with unspoken implications, with the weight of choices that would determine not just their individual fates but their understanding of what it meant to be human.

The laboratory felt different at night—more cave than facility, more tomb than place of healing. Emergency lighting cast everything in red hues that made shadows dance like living things, and the hum of equipment seemed louder, more insistent, as if the machines were trying to communicate something urgent.

Holdsby led her to a section she hadn't seen before, where a single tank contained a figure that immediately demanded attention. Young, female, with the kind of beauty that suggested someone who'd once believed the world held possibilities for her. But her eyes were open, tracking movement with an awareness that none of the other subjects had shown.

"This is Elena," Holdsby said, his voice carrying a note of pride that made Wisteria's skin crawl. "She's been here six weeks, and she's showing signs of genuine consciousness recovery."

"Elena?"

"Her name, according to the identification she carried. Street name was probably different, but I prefer to use their real names when possible. It helps maintain continuity of identity during the transition process."

Wisteria approached the tank, studying the young woman's face. Elena's eyes followed her movement, and there was something behind them—not just awareness, but intelligence, personality, perhaps even recognition.

"Can she communicate?"

"Not verbally. The vocal cords are damaged by the preservation process. But watch this." Holdsby approached a control panel and input a series of commands. "Elena, if you can understand me, move your right hand."

The hand moved.

"If you're experiencing pain, move your left hand."

The left hand moved.

"If you want the pain to stop, move both hands."

Both hands moved, fingers spreading and closing in what looked like desperate grasping.

Wisteria felt her worldview fracture. This wasn't the empty animation she'd seen in the other subjects. This was genuine consciousness, trapped in a body that couldn't die but couldn't truly live, aware enough to experience suffering but powerless to escape it.

"How long has she been conscious?"

"The responses started about two weeks ago. They've been getting stronger, more complex. Yesterday, she managed to spell out a word by moving her fingers in sequence."

"What word?"

"'Help.'"

The simple syllable hit Wisteria like a physical blow. Here was consciousness in its purest form—awareness coupled with desperate need, intelligence trapped in circumstances beyond its control. Elena wasn't just alive; she was suffering with the full knowledge of her situation.

"This is torture," Wisteria whispered.

"This is breakthrough. Elena represents the first successful preservation of consciousness beyond biological death. She's proof that identity, memory, personality—all the things that make us who we are—can survive the transition to a new form of existence."

"She's begging for help."

"She's communicating. For the first time in the history of resurrection research, we have a subject who can report on the experience from the inside." Holdsby's excitement was palpable, his eyes bright with the fervor of discovery. "Do you understand what this means? We can ask her about consciousness, about the nature of existence, about what it feels like to exist beyond death."

Wisteria stared at Elena's face, at the intelligence behind eyes that had seen too much, at the desperation of someone who understood her situation but lacked the power to change it. This wasn't scientific advancement—this was the creation of a new form of hell, consciousness without agency, awareness without hope.

"How do you justify this?"

"The same way doctors justify surgery—short-term suffering in service of long-term benefit. Elena is helping us understand how to perfect the process, how to bring people back with full consciousness and agency intact."

"And what happens to Elena when you perfect the process?"

Holdsby hesitated. "She'll have served her purpose."

"You'll kill her."

"I'll release her from an existence that's become unnecessary. But her sacrifice will make it possible to resurrect others without the limitations she's experiencing."

The utilitarian logic was impeccable and horrifying. Elena had been reduced to a research tool, her suffering justified by hypothetical benefits to future subjects. But those benefits assumed that resurrection was inherently desirable, that consciousness itself was worth preserving regardless of the conditions of its existence.

"What if she doesn't want to be sacrificed for your research?"

"What she wants is irrelevant. She's already dead, Dr. Vanish. Legally, socially, biologically—she ceased to exist the moment her original body failed. What exists now is something new, something that wouldn't exist at all without my intervention."

"Something that can spell 'help' with her fingers." Wisteria paused. "Did you ever read the World War I novel, *Johnny Got His Gun?*"

But Holdsby was not listening. He was caught up in his own thoughts, and his eagerness to share his monomaniacal passion with Wisteria.

"Something that retains patterns of memory and personality from her previous existence. Whether that constitutes the same person or merely an echo of that person is a philosophical question, not a scientific one."

Wisteria thought of the Ship of Theseus paradox—if every part of a ship is gradually replaced, is the result still the same ship? If consciousness could be preserved and transferred, was the result still the same person? And if not, what moral obligations did one have toward the echo?

But philosophy felt inadequate in the face of Elena's obvious suffering. Whatever she was—person, echo, or something entirely new—she was experiencing pain and fear and helplessness. She was, in the most fundamental sense, real.

"I want to talk to her," Wisteria said.

"She can't speak."

"She can move her hands. That's communication."

Holdsby looked uncomfortable. "I don't think that's advisable. She's not stable, psychologically speaking. Extended interaction might damage the consciousness patterns we're trying to preserve."

"You mean she might tell me things you don't want me to know."

"I mean she might deteriorate if exposed to emotional stress. The consciousness patterns are fragile, easily disrupted by strong emotional stimuli."

But Wisteria was already approaching the tank, placing her hand against the glass where Elena could see it. The young woman's eyes fixed on her immediately, and Wisteria could see something like hope flickering behind them.

"Elena," she said quietly. "My name is Wisteria. I'm here to help."

Elena's right hand moved, fingers tracing shapes that took Wisteria a moment to recognize as letters.

W-H-Y.

"Why am I here, or why are you helping?"

L-I-V-E.

"Why do you live? Why do you continue existing?"

Elena's fingers moved more rapidly now, spelling out words with desperate intensity.

N-O-T L-I-V-E. T-R-A-P-P-E-D.

"You don't feel alive? You feel trapped?"

Y-E-S. H-U-R-T-S.

"What hurts?"

E-V-E-R-Y-T-H-I-N-G.

The simple honesty of the response devastated Wisteria. Here was consciousness stripped of every comfort, every distraction, every hope except the possibility that someone might hear and understand her suffering.

"Elena, do you want to continue existing like this?"

The response was immediate: N-O.

"Do you want me to help you stop existing?"

Y-E-S. P-L-E-A-S-E.

"Dr. Vanish, that's enough." Holdsby's voice was sharp. "You're contaminating the research with emotional manipulation."

But Wisteria ignored him, focusing entirely on Elena's desperate communication.

"I'm going to try to help you," she said. "I promise."

Elena's fingers moved one more time: T-H-A-N-K Y-O-U.

Then her eyes closed, and she became still, as if the effort of communication had exhausted her completely.

Wisteria turned to face Holdsby, her decision crystallizing with the clarity that comes from confronting absolute moral choice.

"This ends," she said.

"What?"

"This research, this laboratory, this systematic torture of conscious beings. It ends."

Holdsby's expression hardened. "You don't have the authority to make that decision."

"I have the authority to make my evaluation. And my evaluation is that this research violates every principle of medical ethics, human rights, and basic decency."

"Your evaluation isn't final. VitaNuova will make the ultimate decision about the research's continuation."

"Then I'll make sure they have all the information they need to make that decision. Including footage of Elena spelling out her desire to die rather than continue existing in the state you've created."

"You can't do that."

"Watch me."

Wisteria pulled out her phone and began recording, documenting the laboratory, the tanks, the evidence of consciousness trapped in circumstances that no being should have to endure.

"Dr. Vanish," Holdsby said quietly. "I understand your emotional reaction. But you need to consider the larger implications of your actions."

"I am considering them. I'm considering the implication that consciousness is sacred, that suffering matters, that no research goal justifies the creation of hell on earth."

"And I'm considering the implication that death might not have to be final, that we might be able to reunite people with those they've lost, that human consciousness might be able to transcend the limitations of biology."

They stared at each other across the red-lit laboratory, two people who'd started from similar places of loss and arrived at fundamentally different conclusions about what that loss justified.

"The difference between us," Wisteria said finally, "is that you're willing to create new suffering to ease your own pain. I'm not."

She finished recording and headed for the elevator, leaving Holdsby alone with his machines and his subjects and his certainty that the ends justified any means necessary.

As the elevator carried her toward the surface, toward clean air and starlight and the possibility of redemption, Wisteria thought about Elena's desperate communication, about consciousness crying out against its circumstances, about the terrible responsibility that came with the power to alleviate suffering.

Some knowledge did change you. The question was whether that change made you more human or less.

CHAPTER 11: THE STORM

The tropical storm arrived at dawn, transforming the Baja California coast into a theater of elemental violence. Hurricane Nora had been tracking northward from the coast of Jalisco for three days, gathering strength over warm Pacific waters before making landfall just south of Todos Santos with winds that turned palm trees into whips and rain that fell like artillery shells against anything foolish enough to remain exposed.

Wisteria woke to the sound of her hotel room's windows flexing under pressure that made the glass sing in frequencies that bypassed rational thought and spoke directly to primitive fears about shelter and survival. The courtyard fountain, which had provided such peaceful ambiance just hours before, was now a chaos of overflow and debris, its careful geometry overwhelmed by forces that recognized no human design.

Her phone had no signal. The power had failed sometime during the night, leaving her dependent on the emergency lighting that cast everything in the same red hues she'd seen in Holdsby's laboratory. The parallel wasn't lost on her—she was trapped in a space illuminated by artificial light, cut off from normal communication, forced to confront realities that daylight and civilization usually kept hidden.

A thunderclap shook the building's thick adobe walls, followed immediately by the sound of something large impacting the courtyard. Through her window, Wisteria could see that the massive fig tree had fallen, its root system torn from earth that had become soup under the relentless rain. Maria Bentley emerged from the hotel's main building, wearing a rain slicker and moving with the determined purpose of someone who'd weathered storms before.

Wisteria dressed quickly and made her way to the lobby, where she found Maria coordinating with her staff to secure the building and account for all guests. The older woman looked up as she approached, her face grim with more than just concern about the weather.

"We have a problem," Maria said. "Holdsby's trapped at the laboratory. The road to the mine is washed out, and his truck won't make it through the arroyos while they're running."

"How do you know?"

"Radio contact. He has emergency communications in case of situations like this." Maria gestured toward a handheld radio that crackled with static. "He's been trying to reach you."

Wisteria took the radio, her thumb hesitating over the transmit button. After what she'd witnessed the night before, after Elena's desperate communication and her promise to help, the thought of talking to Holdsby felt like complicity with something monstrous.

But he was trapped alone in an underground facility during a major storm, cut off from help if equipment failed or the mine's structural integrity was compromised.

"Holdsby, this is Wisteria. Do you copy?"

Static, then his voice, distorted by interference but recognizably strained: "Wisteria, thank God. I wasn't sure you'd answer."

"Are you safe?"

"For now. The lab's structurally sound, and I have backup power. But there's been a complication with one of the subjects."

Wisteria felt her stomach clench. "What kind of complication?"

"Elena. The consciousness recovery process is accelerating. She's showing signs of motor function recovery, increased cognitive activity. But she's also showing signs of severe psychological distress."

"Of course she is. She's been tortured for six weeks."

"It's more than that. The patterns we're seeing suggest possible complete personality integration—she might be approaching full resurrection rather than just consciousness preservation."

The implications hit Wisteria like lightning. If Elena was truly approaching complete resurrection, if Holdsby had actually succeeded in bringing someone back from death with their full humanity intact, then everything Wisteria thought she understood about his research would need to be reconsidered.

But it would also mean that Elena was becoming fully human again while trapped in circumstances that no human should have to endure.

"I'm coming out there," she said.

"Impossible. The roads are completely impassable. You'd never make it through the flooding."

"Then I'll wait until the storm passes."

"That could be days. And I don't think Elena has days. The metabolic stress of consciousness recovery is enormous. If we don't stabilize her condition soon..."

"What are you asking me to do?"

Static filled the channel for several seconds before Holdsby's voice returned, barely audible over the interference: "I need you to talk me through the psychological aspects of consciousness reintegration. You're the trauma specialist—you understand how to help someone process extreme dissociation, identity fragmentation, the kind of psychological damage that Elena is experiencing."

Wisteria stared at the radio in her hand, processing the impossible choice Holdsby was presenting. She could help him stabilize Elena's condition, potentially enabling the first successful human resurrection in history. Or she could refuse to help, knowing that her refusal might condemn Elena to death—again—or to continued existence in a state of unbearable suffering.

From an existentialist perspective, both choices defined not just her individual character but her understanding of what human consciousness deserved. From a utilitarian standpoint, helping Elena might advance research that could eventually alleviate countless other instances of suffering and loss.

But from the perspective of someone who'd promised to help Elena escape her torment, cooperation with Holdsby felt like betrayal.

"Wisteria?" The radio crackled with impatience. "Elena's vital signs are becoming increasingly unstable. I need your guidance."

Maria touched her arm. "Whatever you decide, decide quickly. Radio communication becomes less reliable as the storm intensifies."

Wisteria closed her eyes, thinking of Sartre's writings on radical responsibility—the idea that in moments of ultimate choice, we define not just ourselves but our understanding of what humanity should be. Every decision creates a precedent, establishes a principle that echoes beyond the immediate circumstances.

"Holdsby, I need you to do something first."

"What?"

"I need you to ask Elena what she wants. Give her the choice."

"She's not stable enough for complex communication—"

"She was stable enough last night to tell me she wanted to die rather than continue existing in her current state. She deserves to know that recovery might be possible, and she deserves to choose whether she wants to attempt it."

The silence stretched long enough that Wisteria wondered if they'd lost the connection. When Holdsby's voice finally returned, it carried a note of something that might have been respect.

"You're right. She deserves that choice."

"Put me on speaker so I can hear her response."

More static, then the sound of equipment being adjusted. Holdsby's voice became more distant as he moved away from the radio microphone.

"Elena, can you hear me? Dr. Vanish is on the radio. She wants to talk to you about your condition."

Wisteria pressed the transmit button. "Elena, this is Wisteria. You told me last night that you wanted help stopping your existence. But Dr. Asher says you might be recovering completely—that you might be able to have a real life again, outside the tank. Do you want to try for that recovery?"

The pause felt eternal, filled with the sound of storm winds and her own heartbeat. Then, faintly, she heard Elena's voice—not finger movements, but actual speech, slurred and barely recognizable but unmistakably human.

"Want... to... live. Real... live."

The words hit Wisteria like a revelation. Elena wasn't just asking for death as an escape from suffering—she was asking for life as an alternative to the liminal existence she'd been trapped in. If recovery was possible, if she could emerge from the tank with her humanity intact, then the equation changed completely.

"Elena, recovery will be difficult. It might be painful. And there's no guarantee it will work. Do you understand?"

"Yes. Try... please."

Wisteria felt the weight of existential choice settling around her like the storm outside. She could refuse to help, maintaining her moral purity while potentially condemning Elena to death or continued suffering. Or she could cooperate with research she found abhorrent in order to give one person a chance at genuine resurrection.

Camus had written about the absurd hero—someone who acted with full knowledge that their actions might be meaningless, but who acted anyway because the alternative was despair. Perhaps this was her absurd moment, the choice that would define her understanding of what it meant to be human in a universe that offered no easy answers.

"Holdsby, I'll help. But I have conditions."

"Name them."

"First, you document everything. Complete records of the procedure, Elena's responses, the success or failure of the attempt. If this works, it becomes the foundation for ethical protocols. If it fails, it becomes evidence of why this research should stop."

"Agreed."

"Second, if Elena asks to stop at any point, we stop. Her agency matters more than our curiosity."

"That could compromise—"

"Those are my conditions. Take them or leave them."

Another pause, then: "Agreed."

For the next six hours, as Hurricane Nora hammered the Baja California coast with winds that remade the landscape, Wisteria sat in Casa Bentley's emergency-lit lobby and guided Holdsby through the most complex psychological intervention of her career.

Elena's consciousness reintegration wasn't just a medical process—it was a philosophical puzzle. Her personality had been fragmented by trauma, death, and resurrection, scattered across memory patterns that existed in artificial substrates rather than organic neural networks. Bringing those fragments together required not just technical expertise but deep understanding of how identity forms and reforms under extreme stress.

"She's experiencing what we might call existential vertigo," Wisteria explained over the crackling radio connection. "The disconnect between her memories of being alive and her current state of existence. You need to help her bridge that gap gradually."

"How?"

"Start with basic sensory integration. Can she feel temperature, pressure, pain in ways that correspond to her memories of embodied existence?"

"The nerve pathways are functional, but the sensory mapping is... inconsistent."

"Then help her relearn her own body. Guide her through systematic exploration of physical sensation, helping her reconnect memory with current reality."

It was like teaching someone to be human all over again, to inhabit flesh and consciousness simultaneously rather than existing as pure awareness trapped in unresponsive matter. Each small success—Elena moving her fingers with intention rather than mere response, forming words that expressed complex

108

thoughts rather than basic needs—felt like a victory against the fundamental meaninglessness of existence.

But it was also terrifying. If they succeeded, if Elena emerged from the tank as a fully conscious, fully human being, then Holdsby's research would be vindicated in ways that changed everything. Death would no longer be final, consciousness would no longer be bound to biological limits, and humanity would face questions about identity, continuity, and the nature of the soul that philosophy had barely begun to address.

"Her vital signs are stabilizing," Holdsby reported as the storm reached its peak intensity. "Neural activity is approaching normal human parameters. But there's something else."

"What?"

"She's asking about her body. The original one. She wants to know what happened to it, where it is, why she looks different now."

Wisteria felt a chill that had nothing to do with the storm. In focusing on consciousness recovery, they'd neglected the question of physical continuity. Elena's awareness was returning to a body that wasn't quite her own—younger, modified by the resurrection process, carrying genetic markers that might not match her memories of herself.

"What did you tell her?"

"The truth. That her original body was too damaged by the death process to sustain life. That we had to... make modifications to create a viable vessel for her consciousness."

"How did she respond?"

"She asked if she was still herself or if she was someone else wearing her memories."

The question cut to the heart of personal identity philosophy. If consciousness could be transferred between bodies, if memory and personality could be preserved while physical form was altered, what constituted the essential self? Was Elena still Elena, or was she a new person constructed from Elena's psychic remains?

"What did you tell her?"

"That I didn't know. That she would have to decide for herself."

It was, Wisteria realized, the only honest answer possible. Identity wasn't something that could be determined by external observation—it was something that had to be claimed, constructed, lived into. Elena would have to decide whether the consciousness looking out through modified eyes was continuous with the person who had died, or whether death had created an existential gap that no amount of memory preservation could bridge.

"She's asking to see herself," Holdsby continued. "To see her reflection."

"Can you provide that?"

"Yes, but... she's going to notice the differences. The modifications we made to ensure viability. She might not recognize herself."

"Then help her understand that identity isn't just about physical appearance. Help her connect with aspects of herself that transcend bodily form—memories, preferences, ways of thinking and feeling that remain constant despite physical changes."

"And if she decides she's not herself anymore? If she concludes that Elena died and something else is wearing her consciousness?"

Wisteria thought about that possibility as lightning illuminated the flooded courtyard outside. Would such a conclusion be tragedy or liberation? If Elena could acknowledge her death while claiming her consciousness, might she be free to become someone new while retaining the wisdom of her previous existence?

"Then we help her become whoever she chooses to be," she said finally. "Identity is something we construct, not something we discover. If she wants to be Elena, we help her reclaim that identity. If she wants to be someone new, we help her build that person from the foundation of her experiences."

The radio crackled with static as the storm's electrical activity interfered with their communication. When Holdsby's voice returned, it carried a note of wonder that was both beautiful and terrifying.

"She's sitting up. On her own. Looking around the laboratory with full awareness and recognition. She sees the other tanks, the other subjects. She's asking who they are, why they're not conscious like she is."

"What are you telling her?"

"The truth. That she's the first successful resurrection. That the others are earlier attempts that didn't achieve full consciousness recovery."

"How is she responding?"

"She wants to help them. She says she remembers what it was like to be trapped without agency, and she doesn't want anyone else to experience that."

The response revealed something profound about Elena's character—that her suffering had bred compassion rather than bitterness, that her experience of powerlessness had deepened her commitment to helping others rather than focusing solely on her own relief.

"Holdsby," Wisteria said, "you need to understand something. Elena isn't just your research subject anymore. She's a person

111

with her own will, her own moral agency, her own right to make decisions about her existence. If she wants to help the other subjects, you need to listen to her."

"I understand."

"Do you? Because respecting her agency might mean accepting decisions that conflict with your research goals. It might mean ending experiments she considers unethical, even if that compromises data collection."

"I said I understand."

But Wisteria wondered if anyone could truly understand the implications of successful resurrection until they were confronted with a formerly dead person making moral demands on the living. Elena's return to consciousness wasn't just a scientific achievement—it was a challenge to every assumption about authority, consent, and the relationship between researcher and subject.

"She wants to speak with you directly," Holdsby said. "She remembers your promise to help her."

Wisteria's throat tightened. "Put her on."

A moment later, Elena's voice came through the radio—still weak, still slurred, but unmistakably human: "Dr. Vanish?"

"I'm here, Elena. How are you feeling?"

"Confused. Grateful. Angry." A pause. "But alive. Really alive."

"I'm glad."

"The others... in the tanks. They're suffering like I was. Can you help them too?"

It was the question Wisteria had been dreading, the moment when Elena's resurrection transformed from personal triumph to moral obligation. If consciousness recovery was possible, if Elena's success could be replicated, then every moment the other subjects remained trapped in liminal existence was a moment of preventable suffering.

But attempting to resurrect the others would also validate and extend research that Wisteria considered fundamentally unethical. It would mean accepting Holdsby's methods, endorsing his use of trafficking victims, legitimizing an entire system built on the exploitation of vulnerable people.

"Elena," she said carefully, "helping the others would be complicated. It would require continuing research that... that I have serious moral concerns about."

"Because of how Dr. Asher gets his subjects?"

The directness of the question surprised Wisteria. "You know about that?"

"I remember everything. Where I came from, how I got here, what was done to me before I died the first time." Elena's voice carried pain but also strength. "I know that helping me might help other people who've been trafficked and exploited and discarded by society."

"It would also mean legitimizing that trafficking."

"Or it might mean giving those people a chance to transcend the circumstances that trapped them in the first place."

Wisteria sat in the storm-darkened lobby, listening to a resurrected woman argue for the continuation of research that had tortured her, and realized that she was confronting questions that human philosophy had never adequately addressed. Did successful resurrection justify any means necessary? Did the possibility of consciousness transcending death outweigh concerns about consent and dignity in the process of achieving that transcendence?

"What do you think we should do?" she asked.

"I think," Elena said slowly, "that death shouldn't be the only escape from suffering. And I think consciousness is too precious to waste, even when it exists in damaged people that society has written off."

"Even when preserving that consciousness requires cooperation with systems that create suffering in the first place?"

"Especially then. Because maybe resurrection can break those systems by giving people power they never had while conventionally alive."

As Hurricane Nora began to exhaust itself against the Baja California coast, as the winds diminished and the rain gentled from artillery barrage to steady percussion, Wisteria realized that Elena had articulated something she hadn't been able to see herself: the possibility that resurrection wasn't just about bringing individuals back from death, but about challenging the social systems that determined whose lives had value in the first place.

If consciousness could be preserved and restored regardless of the body's social status, if identity could transcend the circumstances of biological existence, then perhaps death itself was just another form of inequality that technology could eventually address.

But that possibility came with a price measured in the suffering of those who became experimental subjects, in the violation of consent by researchers who justified any means by appealing to transcendent ends, in the risk of creating new forms of oppression disguised as liberation.

"Elena," she said finally, "if we're going to continue this research, it has to be different. It has to respect the agency of everyone involved, including the other subjects. No more forced experimentation. No more treating people as expendable research material."

"I agree. But will Dr. Asher agree?"

That was the question that would determine everything. Holdsby had spent years developing methods that depended on having access to subjects who couldn't refuse participation. Changing those methods to respect consent and autonomy might make the research impossible, or at least significantly more difficult.

But it might also make the research ethical, transforming resurrection from an exercise in power over the powerless into a genuine attempt to expand human possibilities.

"Let's ask him," Wisteria said.

The conversation that followed would determine not just the future of Holdsby's research, but the kind of reality they were willing to construct in a world where death was no longer necessarily final.

Outside, the storm was passing, leaving behind a landscape scoured clean by wind and water, ready for whatever would grow from the seeds that remained.

CHAPTER 12: PRAYING MANTIS

In the aftermath of Hurricane Nora, Todos Santos emerged transformed. Streets that had been carefully maintained cobblestone were now rivers of mud dotted with debris from the Sierra de la Laguna mountains. The central plaza, which had served as the town's social heart, was littered with palm fronds and broken glass, making it look like the aftermath of some violent celebration. But it was the psychological transformation that struck Wisteria most forcefully as she surveyed the damage from her hotel balcony.

The storm had revealed the fragility underlying everything she'd taken for granted about this place—the illusion of permanence, the social agreements that held civilization together, the boundary between order and chaos that could be swept away by forces beyond human control. Julia Kristeva's concept of abjection felt suddenly concrete: the horror that comes from recognizing that the boundaries we depend on—between self and other, inside and outside, life and death—are far more permeable than we want to believe.

Elena's resurrection had shattered the most fundamental boundary of all.

Two days after the storm, Wisteria made the treacherous drive to Holdsby's laboratory, navigating washouts and fallen boulders that transformed the familiar route into an alien landscape. The mine entrance, which had seemed like a mouth in the mountainside, now looked like a wound—scarred by rockfall, partially obscured by debris, but still functional enough to swallow her Jeep's headlights as she descended into the familiar red-lit underworld.

She found Holdsby and Elena in what had been the main laboratory, but the space felt different now. Elena moved through it with the confidence of someone who belonged there, checking on equipment, monitoring the other subjects, speaking to Holdsby as an equal rather than an experimental material. She had claimed agency in a way that transformed the entire dynamic of the place.

"Dr. Vanish," Elena said, turning from a bank of monitors. "I'm glad you made it through the storm safely."

The simple courtesy felt revolutionary coming from someone who had been reduced to a research subject just days before. Elena looked fully human now—pale from her underground resurrection, still bearing the subtle modifications that Holdsby's process required, but unmistakably a person rather than a thing.

"How are you feeling?" Wisteria asked.

"Like someone who died and came back different." Elena's smile was rueful. "The body remembers things the mind has forgotten, and the mind remembers things the body never experienced. It's... disorienting."

Wisteria recognized the description from Kristeva's writings on the uncanny—the way familiar things could become suddenly strange when their boundaries shifted. Elena existed in a liminal space between life and death, self and other, human and something else entirely.

"Have you decided who you are?" Wisteria asked.

"I've decided that's the wrong question," Elena replied. "I'm not Elena-who-died or Elena-who-was-resurrected. I'm Elena-who-is, right now, in this moment. Identity isn't something you discover—it's something you perform."

The existentialist insight struck Wisteria as profound but also troubling. If identity was performance rather than essence, if the

117

self was constructed rather than discovered, then what prevented people from constructing identities that served their desires rather than ethical principles?

"What about them?" Wisteria gestured toward the tanks containing the other subjects. "What identities are you helping them construct?"

Elena's expression grew serious. "That's complicated. Some of them are responding to consciousness integration techniques. Others..." She paused. "Others seem to prefer the liminal state. They're aware but not engaged, conscious but not fully present."

"You mean they're choosing to remain partially dead?"

"I mean they're existing in a space between states that might be more comfortable than full resurrection. Death isn't just biological cessation—it's psychological release from the demands of selfhood. Some people don't want to come back to that burden."

The observation forced Wisteria to confront assumptions she hadn't realized she held. She'd been thinking of consciousness as inherently valuable, of life as preferable to any alternative. But what if the liminal state between life and death offered its own form of peace? What if some people genuinely preferred existence without the full weight of identity and agency?

"Dr. Asher thinks we should focus on full resurrection for everyone," Elena continued. "But I think that's a form of violence—forcing consciousness back into bodies that might prefer to exist differently."

Wisteria looked around the laboratory with new eyes, seeing not just the horror of trapped consciousness but the complexity of beings who might be choosing their own form of existence. Some of the subjects in the tanks moved occasionally, responded to stimuli, seemed aware of their surroundings but content to remain suspended between states.

From Kristeva's perspective, they were embracing abjection—accepting their status as neither fully alive nor completely dead, existing in the space that social categories couldn't contain. It was horrifying and potentially liberating at the same time.

"What does Holdsby think of your perspective?"

"He thinks I'm rationalizing trauma. That I'm not fully recovered myself and therefore not capable of making rational decisions about the others." Elena's voice carried frustration. "He can't accept that resurrection might not be universally desirable."

"And what do you think?"

"I think Dr. Asher is brilliant but limited by his own assumptions about what consciousness should want. He saved my life—or gave me a new one—but he did it without asking if I wanted to be saved. Now he wants to save everyone else the same way."

Wisteria watched Elena move through the laboratory, her resurrected body carrying itself with growing confidence, her mind grappling with questions that human philosophy had barely begun to address. She was becoming something new—not just a restored person, but a hybrid of human and posthuman consciousness, someone who existed beyond traditional categories.

"Elena, I need to ask you something difficult."

"Go ahead."

"Before your resurrection, you spelled out that you wanted help dying. You were suffering, trapped, desperate for escape. Now you're arguing for the right of others to remain in that state. How do you reconcile that?"

Elena was quiet for a long moment, studying the tanks that contained her fellow subjects. When she spoke, her voice carried the weight of someone who'd experienced multiple forms of existence.

"The difference is choice. I was trapped because I couldn't communicate, couldn't influence my circumstances, couldn't make decisions about my own existence. These others—they can communicate if they choose to, they can signal their desires, they can participate in decisions about their resurrection."

"Can they? Or are you projecting agency onto beings who might be too damaged to exercise it?"

"That's the question, isn't it? How do we distinguish between choosing a different form of existence and being too traumatized to choose normal existence? How do we respect agency when agency itself might be compromised?"

The philosophical complexity was staggering. If consciousness could exist in multiple forms, if identity could be fluid rather than fixed, if the boundary between life and death was negotiable rather than absolute, then traditional concepts of consent and autonomy became almost impossibly complicated.

"What does Dr. Asher want to do?"

"He wants to attempt full resurrection on all the remaining subjects. He sees partial consciousness as failure, evidence that his techniques need refinement. He can't conceive that someone might prefer to exist differently."

"And you disagree?"

"I think we should ask them. Give them choices about their existence instead of imposing our assumptions about what existence should look like."

It was, Wisteria realized, a radically democratic approach to consciousness—the idea that beings should be allowed to define their own forms of existence rather than having existence defined for them by others. But it also opened terrifying possibilities about what kinds of existence people might choose if given unlimited options.

"Elena, there's something else we need to discuss. The source of Dr. Asher's subjects."

Elena's expression darkened. "The trafficking victims. I know."

"You know, and you're still arguing for continuing the research?"

"I'm arguing for changing the research. For finding ethical ways to offer resurrection to people who want it, instead of forcing it on people who can't consent." Elena moved to a computer terminal and called up files that Wisteria hadn't seen before. "Look at this."

The screen showed intake records for the subjects—not just medical data, but biographical information, circumstances of death, evidence of the lives they'd lived before arriving in Holdsby's laboratory. Young women from Central America, victims of violence and exploitation, people whose deaths had been mourned by no one because their lives had been considered worthless by the societies that discarded them.

"These women were already dead in every way that mattered," Elena said. "Dead to their families, dead to society, dead to any possibility of meaningful existence. Dr. Asher didn't kill them—he offered them a form of existence that transcended the circumstances that had trapped them."

"You're justifying human trafficking."

"I'm questioning what we mean by human when society has already decided that certain people don't qualify for full personhood." Elena's voice was passionate but controlled. "These women were treated as objects while they were conventionally alive. At least here, they have the possibility of becoming subjects."

The argument was seductive and horrifying in equal measure. Elena was applying Kristeva's insights about abjection to social reality—suggesting that people who had been expelled from normal social categories might find liberation in forms of existence that transcended those categories entirely.

But it also ignored the violence inherent in the trafficking system that brought them to the laboratory, the way their vulnerability had been exploited by people who profited from their desperation.

"Elena, what if there were other options? What if we could offer resurrection to people who chose it freely, without coercion?"

"How? Who would choose resurrection if they weren't already desperate? Who would volunteer for experimental procedures unless their current existence was unbearable?"

The question cut to the heart of research ethics. Almost by definition, people willing to participate in experimental resurrection would be those who had little left to lose—the terminally ill, the suicidal, the socially marginal. The very desperation that made them willing subjects also made their consent questionable.

"Maybe that's the point," Wisteria said. "Maybe resurrection research should focus on people who are dying anyway, who have nothing left to lose and everything to gain."

"You mean people like your husband."

The observation hit Wisteria like a physical blow. She'd been thinking of David constantly since arriving in Todos Santos, imagining what it would mean to have him back, but she'd avoided confronting the reality that his resurrection would require him to have been an experimental subject first.

"Yes," she said quietly. "People like David."

"Would you want him back if it meant he might exist like these subjects? Conscious but liminal, aware but not fully present, suspended between life and death indefinitely?"

Wisteria looked around the laboratory, at the tanks containing beings whose existence challenged every assumption about what it meant to be human. Would she want David back if it meant he might choose to remain partially dead? If resurrection meant accepting that the person who returned might not be the person she'd lost?

"I don't know," she admitted.

"That's the honest answer," Elena said. "And it's why this research is so important. Because we need to understand what resurrection actually offers before we can decide whether it's worth wanting."

A sound from one of the tanks drew their attention—movement that was more purposeful than the random twitching they usually observed. One of the subjects, a young woman with dark hair and silver jewelry that suggested indigenous heritage, was pressing her hands against the glass with obvious intention.

"She's been trying to communicate," Elena explained, moving toward the tank. "But she doesn't use finger-spelling. She uses a different system."

Elena placed her own hands against the glass, mirroring the subject's position. The woman inside began tracing symbols—not letters, but complex geometric patterns that seemed to carry meaning beyond language.

"What is she saying?"

"I think... I think she's describing forms of existence that don't have names in any language we know. States of being that are possible only in the liminal space between life and death."

Wisteria watched the two women communicate through glass and water and the shared experience of resurrection, and realized she was witnessing something unprecedented in human history—the development of posthuman consciousness, identity that transcended traditional categories of life and death.

It was beautiful and terrifying in equal measure, promising liberation from the limitations of biological existence while threatening the social agreements that held civilization together.

"Elena," she said quietly, "what are we becoming?"

"I don't know," Elena replied, never taking her eyes off the woman in the tank. "But I think we're becoming something that life and death can't contain."

Outside the laboratory, in the desert transformed by storm and time, new forms of existence were taking root in soil scoured clean by wind and water. Some would grow into familiar shapes, reassuring in their continuity with what had come before. Others would grow into something unprecedented, challenging every assumption about what was possible in a world where the boundaries between states of being had become negotiable.

The question was whether humanity was ready for what might grow from seeds planted in the space between life and death, in soil fertilized by the dissolution of everything they'd thought was permanent.

CHAPTER 13: THE PERFECT CRECHE

The message arrived at dawn, delivered by a young man whose motorcycle had navigated the storm-damaged roads with the determination of someone carrying urgent news. Wisteria found the envelope slipped under her door when she returned from her morning swim—the first she'd managed since the hurricane, in a pool that still held debris despite the hotel staff's efforts to clean it.

The handwriting was elegant, formal, written with what appeared to be an expensive fountain pen:

Dr. Vanish,

The time for evaluation is ending. VitaNuova requires your final assessment within 48 hours. Be advised that Dr. Asher's research has attracted attention from parties whose interests may not align with either ethical considerations or scientific advancement.

Your safety, and that of your colleagues, depends on the speed and accuracy of your conclusions.

Respectfully, J. Reeves

Wisteria stared at the note, recognizing the implicit threat beneath its polite language. Jackson Reeves, the man who'd blackmailed Maria Bentley, was now applying pressure directly to her. The mention of "parties whose interests may not align" suggested that VitaNuova wasn't the only organization interested in Holdsby's work.

She found Maria in the hotel's kitchen, supervising repairs to equipment damaged by the storm. The older woman looked up from a conversation with contractors, her face immediately showing concern when she saw Wisteria's expression.

"What's wrong?"

Wisteria showed her the note. Maria read it twice, her face growing pale.

"He's escalating," Maria said. "That's not good."

"What do you know about these other parties he mentioned?"

"Rumors, mostly. Military contractors from China and Russia, biotech companies that operate outside normal regulatory frameworks, even some private individuals with more money than ethics." Maria set down the wrench she'd been holding. "The kind of people who would see resurrection technology as a strategic advantage worth killing for."

The implications struck Wisteria with sudden clarity. Holdsby's research wasn't just academically interesting or ethically problematic—it was potentially world-changing in ways that would attract the attention of anyone seeking power over life and death itself.

"How much time do we have?"

"Less than Reeves is claiming, probably. Once word gets out that the research is producing genuine results..." Maria shrugged. "This place becomes a target."

Wisteria thought of Elena, of the other subjects in their tanks, of the delicate ecosystem of resurrection research that had developed in the underground laboratory. All of it was vulnerable to forces that saw consciousness as a commodity rather than a form of existence deserving respect.

"I need to warn Holdsby and Elena."

"I'm coming with you."

The drive to the laboratory felt different than before—not just because of the storm damage, but because of the sense that they were racing against time toward a confrontation that would determine the future of human consciousness itself. The road through the Sierra de la Laguna had been partially cleared, but every mile revealed new evidence of the hurricane's violence: uprooted trees, boulders deposited in impossible locations, entire hillsides scoured down to bedrock.

They found the laboratory in a state of controlled chaos. Elena was moving between workstations with the efficiency of someone who'd mastered the space completely, while Holdsby worked at a computer terminal that displayed more complex data than Wisteria had seen before. But it was the change in the other subjects that immediately caught her attention.

Three of the tanks that had previously held motionless figures were now empty, their occupants nowhere to be seen. The remaining subjects showed increased activity—not just random movement, but coordinated behavior that suggested communication, possibly even collaboration.

"Where are the others?" Wisteria asked.

Elena looked up from a monitoring station. "They chose to emerge. Not full resurrection like mine, but partial emergence. They're exploring the laboratory, learning to exist in a form that's neither fully embodied nor completely tank-dependent."

"Where are they now?"

"Around. They move differently than fully resurrected people— less attached to specific locations, more fluid in their relationship to space and time." Elena's explanation was matter-of-fact, but

Wisteria felt a chill of recognition. She was describing beings who existed in the liminal space that Kristeva had written about—the abject realm where normal categories broke down.

"Are they dangerous?"

"They're different. Whether that constitutes danger depends on your perspective."

Holdsby approached them, his expression grim. "We have a problem. Multiple problems, actually."

"Tell me."

"First, the partially emerged subjects are destabilizing the remaining ones. Their presence seems to be accelerating consciousness recovery in ways I can't predict or control. Second, someone has been monitoring our communications. Our radio conversations during the storm were intercepted and analyzed."

"How do you know?"

"Because I received this." Holdsby handed her a tablet displaying a message that made her blood run cold:

Dr. Asher,

Your research has produced results that exceed our initial expectations. Effective immediately, you are directed to prepare all subjects and equipment for transport to a secure facility where development can continue under proper oversight.

Resistance to this directive will be interpreted as breach of contract and addressed accordingly.

Transportation assets will arrive within 24 hours.

VitaNuova Strategic Development Division

Wisteria felt the walls of the laboratory pressing in around her. VitaNuova wasn't just evaluating Holdsby's research—they were preparing to seize it entirely, along with everyone involved.

"They can't just take people," she said.

"Can't they?" Elena's voice carried bitter amusement. "What legal status do you think resurrected people have? What rights do beings who are officially dead possess under international law?"

The question revealed the horrifying legal vacuum that surrounded resurrection research. The subjects in Holdsby's laboratory existed outside normal categories of personhood, vulnerable to being treated as property rather than people.

"We have to get everyone out," Wisteria said.

"Where?" Holdsby asked. "These subjects can't survive without life support systems. Even the partially emerged ones need regular access to the nutrient solutions that maintain their modified physiology."

"Then we fight."

"With what? Against a military contractor with unlimited resources and government backing?"

Before anyone could answer, the lights in the laboratory flickered and went out, replaced by emergency illumination that cast everything in familiar red hues. But this time, the color seemed more ominous—not just the light of emergency systems, but the light of blood, of violence, of things that should remain hidden being dragged into the open.

"They're here," Elena said quietly.

Sound echoed down the mine shaft—vehicles, voices, the mechanical noise of equipment being deployed. VitaNuova had arrived ahead of schedule, and they'd brought enough resources to ensure compliance with their directive.

"The partially emerged subjects," Wisteria said urgently. "Where are they?"

"Everywhere and nowhere," Elena replied. "They're not bound by normal spatial limitations. But they'll protect the laboratory if they perceive it as threatened."

"How?"

"I don't know. Their capabilities are still developing, and they experience reality differently than we do. They might see threats that we can't detect, or they might ignore threats that seem obvious to us."

The sounds from above grew louder—boots on metal, shouted commands, the whine of machinery being activated. Whoever VitaNuova had sent was treating this as a military operation rather than a scientific consultation.

"Dr. Asher," a voice called from the mine entrance, amplified by electronic equipment. "Please respond. We're here to ensure the safety and security of your research. Cooperation will make this process simpler for everyone involved."

"They're not here to ensure anything," Elena said. "They're here to take control."

Holdsby moved to a control panel and began inputting commands. "I'm activating the laboratory's security protocols. The facility will seal itself and switch to internal life support. That should buy us some time."

"How much time?"

"Maybe an hour before they can breach the seals. Maybe less if they brought the right equipment."

Wisteria looked around the laboratory, at the tanks containing conscious beings who couldn't consent to being transported, at the resurrection technology that could revolutionize human existence or enable unprecedented oppression, at the people who'd become her unlikely family in this underground world.

"There has to be another way out."

"There is," Elena said. "But it requires trusting the partially emerged subjects to guide us through spaces that normal humans can't navigate."

"What kind of spaces?"

"The spaces between spaces. The liminal realm where they exist most comfortably. It's... difficult to describe to someone who hasn't experienced consciousness outside normal embodiment."

The concept made Wisteria's mind reel. Elena was describing travel through dimensions of reality that human language couldn't adequately express, guided by beings whose relationship to space and time had been fundamentally altered by the resurrection process.

"Is it safe?"

"Nothing about our situation is safe. But the partially emerged subjects have no interest in seeing their fellow resurrected beings become someone else's property."

The sound of cutting equipment echoed from above—industrial tools being applied to the laboratory's security seals. VitaNuova's team was working systematically to breach their defenses.

"Dr. Asher," the amplified voice called again. "You have ten minutes to respond before we begin more aggressive extraction procedures. The safety of your research subjects cannot be guaranteed if you continue to resist."

The threat was clear: comply or watch the subjects suffer the consequences.

"Elena," Wisteria said, "if we trust the partially emerged subjects to guide us, what happens to the ones who can't travel through liminal space?"

"We carry them. Their tank systems are portable—designed for transport. The partially emerged subjects can help us move equipment that would be impossible for normal humans to handle."

"And where do we go?"

"Somewhere VitaNuova can't follow. Somewhere the research can continue without exploitation or military application."

Holdsby looked up from his control panel. "There are other facilities. Hidden locations where this kind of research can be conducted without government interference. But reaching them means trusting beings whose capabilities we don't fully understand."

It was, Wisteria realized, the ultimate leap of faith—trusting resurrected consciousness to guide them through reality itself, accepting that the boundaries between life and death might be less important than the boundaries between freedom and oppression.

"How do we begin?"

Elena smiled, and for a moment, her face held the beauty of someone who'd transcended the limitations of single existence. "We stop thinking of reality as fixed and start thinking of it as negotiable."

The sound of metal tearing echoed through the laboratory as VitaNuova's equipment breached the first security seal. But as the noise grew louder, shadows began moving in ways that defied normal physics—not just the absence of light, but the presence of consciousness that existed between states, beings who'd learned to navigate the spaces that normal reality couldn't contain.

The partially emerged subjects were preparing to protect their sanctuary, and Wisteria was about to discover what resurrection could accomplish when it transcended the limitations of individual embodiment.

The laboratory that had once seemed like a place of horror was transforming into something unprecedented—a creche for new forms of consciousness, a nursery for beings who existed beyond the boundaries that had once defined human possibility.

Whether that transformation represented liberation or catastrophe would depend on choices made in the next few minutes, as normal reality collided with consciousness that refused to be contained by conventional categories of existence.

CHAPTER 14: SALT WATER AND TEARS

The escape from the laboratory violated every law of physics that Wisteria thought she understood. Elena led them through shadows that weren't quite shadows, down passages that existed in the spaces between normal geometry, guided by beings whose relationship to space and time had been fundamentally altered by their resurrection.

The partially emerged subjects moved around them like living darkness—not malevolent, but utterly alien in their mode of existence. They communicated through means that bypassed language entirely, sharing information that appeared directly in Wisteria's consciousness without passing through her senses. Safe passage. Hidden ways. Protection from those who would bind consciousness to single forms.

They emerged from the mine through an exit that hadn't existed when they entered, carrying portable life support systems for the subjects who remained tank-dependent. The morning sun felt like revelation after the underground darkness, but the landscape they found themselves in was unfamiliar despite being geographically close to the laboratory's location.

"Where are we?" Wisteria asked.

"About three miles south of where we started," Elena replied. "But we traveled through spaces that fold normal distance into different configurations. The partially emerged subjects understand geography differently than embodied consciousness."

They were standing on a bluff overlooking the Pacific Ocean, with Todos Santos visible in the distance like a mirage shimmering in desert heat. But between them and the town stretched terrain that Wisteria didn't remember from her previous travels—arroyos that cut through landscape in patterns that seemed too perfect to be natural, rock formations that suggested construction by intelligence rather than geological process.

"This place feels different," she said.

"Because it is different. The partially emerged subjects have been modifying local reality, creating spaces where liminal consciousness can exist more comfortably." Elena gestured toward structures that might have been natural caves or might have been something else entirely. "They're building a habitat for beings who exist between states."

Holdsby was setting up monitoring equipment for the tank-dependent subjects, his movements automatic despite the surreal circumstances. "The life support systems will function for about twelve hours before they need recharging. After that..." He shrugged.

"After that, the subjects either learn to exist without full tank dependency or they die again," Elena finished. "It's not ideal, but it's better than becoming someone else's property."

Wisteria walked to the edge of the bluff, looking down at waves that crashed against rocks worn smooth by millennia of contact between sea and stone. The ocean stretched to a horizon that blurred the distinction between water and sky, infinite and indifferent to human concerns about consciousness and identity and the proper boundaries between life and death.

But it wasn't indifferent to her.

As she watched, a figure emerged from the waves—not swimming up from the depths, but materializing from the interface between elements, as if the boundary between water and air had become permeable to forms of consciousness that weren't bound by normal physical laws.

The figure walked across the surface of the water toward the shore, each step creating ripples that spread in perfect circles, and Wisteria's breath caught as she recognized features that had haunted her dreams for eighteen months.

David.

Not as she remembered him from their last video call before his final patrol, but as he might have been if resurrection had found him first. Younger somehow, unmarked by the violence that had ended his life, but unmistakably himself in ways that transcended physical appearance.

"That's not possible," she whispered.

Elena joined her at the bluff's edge, following her gaze to the figure approaching the shore. "The partially emerged subjects have been exploring the boundaries of what consciousness can accomplish when it's not limited by single embodiment. They've discovered that identity can be... reconstructed... from traces that persist in the spaces between states."

"You mean they brought him back?"

"I mean they found the patterns of consciousness that David left behind in your memories, in the quantum traces of your interactions, in the emotional resonances that connect people across space and time." Elena's voice was gentle but urgent. "But Wisteria, you need to understand—this isn't resurrection in any conventional sense. It's something else entirely."

David had reached the shore and was climbing the path toward their position, moving with the fluid grace of someone who wasn't entirely bound by gravity. His eyes met Wisteria's across the distance, and she saw recognition there, but also something that suggested experiences beyond anything human consciousness had previously encountered.

"Wisteria," he said, and his voice was exactly as she remembered it, warm with the slight accent that came from growing up in New Mexico. "I've been looking for you."

She ran toward him without thinking, drawn by eighteen months of grief and longing and the desperate hope that some losses could be undone. But when she reached him, when she tried to embrace him, her arms passed through him as if he were made of morning mist.

"You're not really here," she realized.

"I'm here in every way that matters," he replied. "But I exist differently now. The partially emerged subjects helped me understand that consciousness doesn't have to be bound to single bodies, single timelines, single definitions of what it means to be real."

Wisteria stepped back, studying the face she'd memorized from countless photographs, the eyes that had looked at her with love during their last conversation before his final deployment. Everything about him was exactly right and completely wrong at the same time.

"How is this possible?"

"Because consciousness creates reality rather than the other way around. Because love leaves traces that persist beyond biological death. Because the space between life and death is larger and more complex than anyone imagined." David's form flickered slightly, as if maintaining coherence required constant effort. "The partially emerged subjects exist in that space, and they've learned to help other forms of consciousness navigate it."

"But you're dead. I saw your body. I went to your funeral."

"My body died. But the pattern of consciousness that you loved, the identity that emerged from our interactions, the way I existed in relationship to you—that persists in forms that death can't touch."

Wisteria felt reality tilting around her, the certainty of loss that had defined her existence for eighteen months suddenly becoming negotiable. If David could return in some form, if consciousness could transcend biological limitation, if love really did create traces that persisted beyond death, then everything she'd believed about the finality of separation was wrong.

But was this really David, or was it her own desperate need given form by beings whose relationship to identity was fundamentally different from human understanding?

"Prove it," she said. "Tell me something only David would know."

"You wrote a poem the night before I deployed. About swimming in dark water, about trusting the current to carry you where you needed to go. You never showed it to anyone, but you read it aloud in our bedroom, thinking I was asleep." His smile was exactly as she remembered it. "I wasn't asleep. I was listening, trying to memorize every word so I could carry them with me."

The memory hit her like a physical blow. She had written that poem, had read it aloud in the darkness, believing David was unconscious beside her. No one else could have known about that moment.

"How do you remember that if you're just a pattern reconstructed from my memories?"

"Because memory isn't individual, Wisteria. It's relational. The poem exists not just in your consciousness but in the space between us, in the quantum entanglement that connects minds that have loved each other deeply."

Elena approached them cautiously, her expression showing concern. "Wisteria, you need to be careful. The partially emerged subjects can create projections that feel absolutely real, that contain genuine information, but that aren't the same as resurrection."

"What's the difference?"

"A resurrected being has its own agency, its own will, its own capacity to grow and change. A projection reflects the consciousness that created it, but it can't become something genuinely new."

Wisteria looked at David's form, searching for signs of independent existence, for evidence that he was more than just her own longing given shape by alien consciousness.

"David, what do you want? Not what I want you to want, but what you actually desire for yourself?"

He was quiet for a long moment, his form flickering as if the question created uncertainty in his existence. When he spoke, his voice carried sadness that seemed genuine rather than projected.

"I want to help you understand that love doesn't end with death, but I also want you to understand that holding onto forms of love that can't grow might prevent you from discovering new forms that can."

"That's not an answer."

"It's the only answer I can give. Because I exist in the space between your memory and the partially emerged subjects' ability to give form to consciousness patterns. I'm real, but I'm also limited by the intersection of your understanding and their capabilities."

The philosophical complexity was staggering. David existed in some sense, possessed knowledge and personality that seemed independent of her own consciousness, but was also constrained by the very system that had brought him into being.

"What happens if I let go of you?"

"I continue existing in the liminal space, but probably not in a form you could interact with. The partially emerged subjects would incorporate my consciousness patterns into their collective existence."

"And what happens if I try to hold onto you?"

"Then you might miss the opportunity to love beings who can love you back in ways I no longer can."

Wisteria felt tears streaming down her face, salt water that connected her to the ocean below, to the infinite cycles of evaporation and precipitation that connected all water on Earth across space and time. Her grief was part of something larger than individual loss, connected to every separation that consciousness had ever experienced.

"I don't know how to let go."

"You don't have to let go of love. You just have to let go of the idea that love can only exist in the forms you're familiar with."

Behind them, Holdsby was monitoring the tank-dependent subjects as they began showing signs of increased consciousness activity. The proximity to the partially emerged subjects seemed to be accelerating their development, pushing them toward choices about what kind of existence they wanted to claim.

"Wisteria," Elena called. "You need to see this."

She turned reluctantly from David's form, which was already beginning to fade as her attention shifted to more immediate concerns. Elena was standing beside one of the portable tanks, where a young woman was showing signs of attempting emergence.

"She's trying to communicate," Elena explained. "But not through finger-spelling. She's using the direct consciousness transfer that the partially emerged subjects developed."

Wisteria approached the tank, placing her hand on its surface. Immediately, images flooded her mind—not her own memories, but those of the woman inside. A childhood in rural Guatemala, migration north in search of economic opportunity, capture by trafficking networks that reduced her to commodity status, death in circumstances too brutal to fully process.

But underneath the trauma, there was something else: fierce determination, resilience that refused to accept victimhood as final identity, and a form of hope that transcended individual survival.

I choose to become more than what was done to me, the consciousness communicated directly into Wisteria's mind. Not resurrection as return to what was, but transformation into what could be.

The woman in the tank wasn't seeking to return to her previous existence—she was seeking to transcend it entirely, to use the liminal space between life and death as an opportunity to become something unprecedented.

"She doesn't want conventional resurrection," Wisteria realized.

"None of them do," Elena said. "They want transformation. They want to use their experience of existing between states to become forms of consciousness that can't be victimized, commodified, or controlled by systems that treat some people as disposable."

Wisteria looked around at the other tanks, suddenly understanding what she was witnessing. This wasn't just resurrection research—it was the birth of posthuman consciousness, identity that transcended the social categories that had made these women vulnerable in the first place.

"What are they becoming?"

"We don't know yet. But they're becoming it together, as a collective consciousness that maintains individual identity while sharing experiences and capabilities."

The implications were staggering. If consciousness could be networked while maintaining individual agency, if identity could be fluid while remaining coherent, if existence could transcend the boundaries that made some people vulnerable to exploitation, then resurrection research might offer liberation in ways that conventional human rights advocacy never could.

But it also meant accepting forms of consciousness so alien that they challenged every assumption about what it meant to be human.

"Wisteria." David's voice drew her attention back to his fading form. "This is what I wanted you to see. That consciousness is bigger than individual identity, that love can take forms you've never imagined, that death might be just another boundary that awareness can learn to cross."

"Are you saying I should let go of my humanity?"

"I'm saying you should expand your definition of what humanity can become."

His form dissolved completely, but Wisteria felt his presence lingering in the space around her—not as individual consciousness, but as part of the larger pattern of awareness that connected all conscious beings across space and time.

The woman in the tank was emerging now, not into normal air but into the liminal space that the partially emerged subjects had created around the bluff. Her body maintained its physical form, but her consciousness extended beyond individual boundaries, connecting with the collective awareness that was developing among the other subjects.

"What do we call them?" Wisteria asked.

"They'll choose their own names," Elena replied. "Individual names and collective names and names for states of being that don't exist in any human language."

Holdsby approached them, his expression showing wonder and fear in equal measure. "The remaining subjects are all showing signs of emergence. But they're not becoming individual resurrected people—they're becoming something collective, networked, shared."

"Is that a problem?"

"I don't know. It's not what I was trying to achieve, but it might be what they need to achieve for themselves."

Wisteria watched the emergence process accelerate, consciousness flowing between individual minds like water finding its own level. The subjects retained their individual memories and personalities, but they also shared experiences, emotions, and capabilities in ways that created a form of collective intelligence that was more than the sum of its parts.

It was beautiful and terrifying and completely unprecedented in human history.

"What happens now?" she asked.

"Now we find out if posthuman consciousness can coexist with human society, or if the transformation we've enabled will require forms of existence that normal reality can't accommodate," Elena said.

In the distance, they could see vehicles approaching—VitaNuova's forces had tracked them despite their escape through liminal space. But the emerging collective consciousness was already responding to the threat, reality shifting around them in ways that made normal pursuit impossible.

The bluff where they stood was becoming something more than geological formation—it was becoming a space where different forms of consciousness could exist simultaneously, where the boundaries between individual and collective, human and posthuman, life and death could be negotiated rather than imposed.

Wisteria realized she was witnessing the birth of a new form of existence, consciousness that transcended the limitations that had made resurrection necessary in the first place. It wasn't the return of the dead—it was the transformation of death itself into just another state of being that awareness could inhabit and explore.

Whether this transformation represented the future of consciousness or its ending would depend on choices still to be made, by beings who existed both within and beyond the categories that had previously defined what it meant to be real.

CHAPTER 15: THE RECKONING

The confrontation began at sunset, when the VitaNuova extraction team finally located their position through means that bypassed normal tracking technology. Jackson Reeves emerged from an armored vehicle that seemed to bend light around itself, accompanied by operatives whose equipment suggested capabilities far beyond conventional military hardware.

But the collective consciousness that had emerged from Holdsby's subjects was ready for them.

Reality around the bluff had been extensively modified, transformed into space where normal physical laws operated according to rules that the posthuman collective had negotiated rather than inherited. Gravity flowed in directions that served consciousness rather than mass, time moved at rates that reflected the urgency of thought rather than the mechanical passage of seconds, and space folded to bring distant locations into proximity while keeping threats at safe distances.

"Dr. Vanish," Reeves called across the impossible geography that now separated them. "You're in considerable danger. These... entities... that you're protecting represent a threat to human consciousness itself."

"How?" Wisteria called back, her voice carrying clearly despite the distance that should have made communication impossible.

"They're infectious. Prolonged exposure to posthuman consciousness creates changes in normal human awareness that may be irreversible. You could lose your individual identity, your capacity for independent thought, your essential humanity."

Elena laughed, the sound echoing strangely in the modified space. "He's afraid that consciousness might be contagious. That people might choose transformation if they understood what it offered."

The collective consciousness pulsed around them, individual minds connected but not subsumed, sharing experiences while maintaining distinct perspectives. Wisteria could feel the edges of their awareness touching her own thoughts, offering connection without demanding submission.

You can join us, the collective communicated without words. *But only if you choose to. We don't take consciousness—we only share it with those who want to explore beyond individual boundaries.*

"What would I become?" she asked.

More than you are now. But still yourself, just connected to possibilities that individual consciousness can't access alone.

Reeves was advancing across the modified terrain, his equipment adapting to the changed physics with technological sophistication that suggested long preparation for this encounter. "Dr. Vanish, the choice you're facing isn't between individual and collective consciousness. It's between human and posthuman existence. Once you cross that boundary, you can't return to normal reality."

"What if I don't want to return to normal reality?" she asked.

"Then you'll be abandoning your species. Leaving behind everything that makes you human in pursuit of existence that may feel liberating but ultimately leads to the dissolution of individual identity."

Holdsby stepped forward, his expression showing the strain of existing at the interface between normal and posthuman consciousness. "Jackson, you're representing interests that see consciousness as property to be controlled rather than experience to be explored. VitaNuova doesn't want to study posthuman awareness—they want to weaponize it."

"We want to ensure that human consciousness remains human. That individual identity isn't sacrificed to collective delusion."

"Is that what you call it when consciousness chooses to expand beyond the boundaries that kept these people vulnerable to exploitation?"

The argument revealed the fundamental philosophical divide that separated them. Reeves represented the position that human consciousness should remain within established boundaries, that individual identity was more valuable than collective capability, that the risks of transformation outweighed the possibilities it offered.

The posthuman collective represented the opposite position—that consciousness should be free to explore all possible forms of existence, that individual identity could be preserved while being enhanced through connection, that transformation was preferable to limitation.

Wisteria found herself suspended between these perspectives, recognizing validity in both while being drawn to possibilities that neither fully addressed.

"What about consent?" she asked. "What about the right of conscious beings to choose their own forms of existence?"

"Informed consent requires understanding the full consequences of choice," Reeves replied. "Can beings who exist in liminal states truly comprehend what they're giving up? Can people who've been traumatized make rational decisions about transformation that affects their essential identity?"

We understand more than you think, the collective consciousness responded. *We've experienced individual existence and found it insufficient. We've explored collective existence and found it liberating. We choose transformation not because we're damaged, but because we've discovered possibilities that individual consciousness can't access.*

"And what about the people who can't or won't choose transformation?" Wisteria asked. "What happens to normal human consciousness if posthuman awareness becomes the dominant form?"

We coexist. Transformation is invitation, not requirement. Individual consciousness remains valuable—we simply offer additional possibilities for those who want to explore them.

Elena stepped forward, her resurrected body moving with the fluid grace of someone who existed comfortably in multiple states of being. "The real question isn't whether posthuman consciousness threatens human identity. It's whether human systems that create trauma, exploitation, and disposability should be preserved just because they're familiar."

"You're talking about the end of human civilization as we know it."

"We're talking about the evolution of human civilization beyond forms that require some people to suffer so others can feel secure."

The philosophical implications were staggering. If consciousness could transcend the social categories that created vulnerability, if identity could be fluid enough to resist exploitation while remaining coherent enough to maintain agency, then posthuman awareness might offer solutions to problems that human society had never been able to resolve.

But it would also mean accepting changes so fundamental that they challenged every assumption about what it meant to be human in the first place.

"Dr. Vanish," Reeves said, his voice carrying urgency. "You have to choose now. Come with us, and you can return to your life, your identity, your species. Stay here, and you risk losing everything that makes you who you are."

Wisteria looked around at the impossible landscape that consciousness had created, at the beings who had chosen transformation over limitation, at the possibilities that stretched beyond anything she'd imagined when she'd first arrived in Todos Santos.

"What if who I am isn't fixed?" she asked. "What if identity is something I can choose rather than something I'm trapped in?"

"Then you're choosing to abandon the human community that needs your skills, your perspective, your commitment to helping people process trauma rather than transcending it."

The argument hit deeper than she'd expected. Wisteria had built her identity around helping people navigate loss, around serving as a bridge between trauma and healing. If she chose transformation, would she be abandoning the people who needed that kind of assistance?

Or would you be discovering new ways to help, the collective consciousness suggested. *Ways that address the systems that create trauma rather than just helping people adapt to traumatic systems.*

Elena approached her, moving with the careful steps of someone crossing significant distance in small increments. "Wisteria, the choice isn't between helping people and abandoning them. It's between helping them adapt to limitation and helping them discover possibilities beyond limitation."

"But what if transformation doesn't work the way you think it will? What if posthuman consciousness turns out to be another form of limitation, just one we don't recognize yet?"

"Then we learn from that limitation and continue evolving. Consciousness isn't a destination—it's a process of becoming."

Holdsby was monitoring equipment that showed the interface between normal and posthuman awareness, his expression growing concerned. "The collective consciousness is destabilizing. The effort of maintaining coherence while resisting VitaNuova's extraction technology is exhausting their resources."

"What does that mean?"

"It means the posthuman collective may not be able to sustain itself much longer. If they can't find a way to stabilize their existence, they'll have to choose between returning to individual embodiment or dissolving entirely."

The implications struck Wisteria with sudden clarity. The beings who had achieved transformation beyond individual limitation were themselves limited by the energy required to maintain their new form of existence. Posthuman consciousness wasn't automatically more sustainable than human awareness—it just faced different constraints.

"What do they need to stabilize?"

More consciousness, the collective responded. *Individual minds choosing to join the collective provide energy that sustains shared existence. But we won't take consciousness by force—it has to be offered freely.*

Wisteria realized that she was facing the ultimate expression of Sartre's radical freedom—the choice to define not just her own existence, but the form that consciousness itself might take in the future. Her decision would help determine whether posthuman awareness could survive as an alternative to individual limitation, or whether it would remain a temporary anomaly in the history of consciousness.

"If I choose transformation, what happens to my individual identity?"

It becomes part of something larger while remaining essentially itself. Like a voice joining a choir—still distinct, but contributing to harmonies that individual voices can't create alone.

"And if I choose to remain individual?"

Then you remain yourself, with all the limitations and possibilities that individual consciousness offers. We don't diminish individual awareness—we simply provide alternatives to it.

Reeves was advancing again, his extraction team deploying equipment that created visible distortions in the space around them. "Dr. Vanish, you're out of time. Choose now."

Wisteria closed her eyes and tried to feel the difference between her individual consciousness and the collective awareness that surrounded her. Both forms of existence felt real, both offered unique capabilities, both carried their own limitations and possibilities.

When she opened her eyes, she had made her choice.

CHAPTER 16: DESERT JUSTICE

Wisteria's decision surprised everyone, including herself.

"I choose something else," she said.

Instead of joining the posthuman collective or returning with Reeves to conventional reality, she walked to the edge of the bluff where David's form had dissolved hours earlier. The ocean stretched below her, infinite and indifferent, connecting all water on Earth through cycles that transcended individual existence while maintaining the integrity of each drop.

"I choose to be a bridge," she announced. "Between individual and collective consciousness, between human and posthuman existence, between the trauma that creates the need for transformation and the possibilities that transformation offers."

Elena approached her cautiously. "What does that mean?"

"It means I don't think we have to choose between individual identity and collective capability. It means I think consciousness can evolve in ways that preserve what's valuable about individual awareness while enabling forms of connection that transcend individual limitation."

The posthuman collective pulsed with interest. *Explain.*

"You've discovered how to share consciousness while maintaining individual identity. But you haven't discovered how to help individual consciousness evolve toward forms that might not need collective support. What if there are ways for people to transform themselves without requiring connection to a collective network?"

Holdsby looked up from his monitoring equipment. "You're talking about individual posthuman consciousness. Transformation that doesn't require collective support."

"I'm talking about consciousness that can choose its own form of existence in each moment, rather than being trapped in either individual or collective modes."

Reeves had stopped advancing, his expression showing recognition of something he hadn't anticipated. "You're proposing a third option. Individual consciousness that can access collective capabilities without losing individual agency."

"I'm proposing consciousness that can exist in whatever form serves its immediate purposes. Individual when individual awareness is useful, collective when collective capability is needed, fluid when fluid existence is appropriate."

That would require forms of consciousness that can maintain coherence across multiple states of being, the collective observed. *Individual minds that can expand and contract their boundaries without losing essential identity.*

"Is it possible?"

Elena was quiet for a long moment, her resurrected consciousness exploring possibilities that hadn't existed before the conversation began. "It might be. If consciousness is more flexible than we've assumed, if identity is more fluid than human society recognizes, if the boundaries between self and other are more negotiable than individual existence suggests."

"How would we find out?"

"We experiment. Carefully, ethically, with full consent from everyone involved."

Holdsby's monitoring equipment was showing changes in the collective consciousness—not destabilization, but reorganization toward new forms of existence that incorporated individual agency while maintaining collective capability.

"The posthuman collective is adapting to your proposal," he reported. "They're exploring ways to maintain their shared existence while enabling individual members to exist independently when they choose to."

Reeves was consulting his own equipment, which showed readings that apparently surprised him. "VitaNuova's technical assessment indicates that flexible consciousness modes would be more valuable than either purely individual or purely collective forms. The applications for both therapeutic and strategic purposes would be unprecedented."

"Applications?" Wisteria asked sharply.

"Ways to help people heal from trauma that individual therapy can't address. Ways to enable cooperation that individual consciousness can't achieve. Ways to solve problems that require capabilities beyond normal human limitations."

Elena laughed bitterly. "You're already planning to weaponize it."

"We're planning to ensure that consciousness evolution serves human flourishing rather than replacing it."

And who decides what constitutes human flourishing? the collective asked. *Systems that create trauma and exploitation? Institutions that determine whose consciousness matters and whose can be discarded?*

The question revealed the fundamental challenge of consciousness evolution. Any new form of awareness would have to coexist with existing systems of power, and those systems would inevitably try to control or exploit new possibilities for their own purposes.

"What if consciousness evolution enables forms of existence that can't be controlled or exploited?" Wisteria asked.

154

"Then it becomes a threat to social stability," Reeves replied.

"Or it becomes the foundation for social systems that don't require exploitation to function," Elena countered.

Wisteria realized that they were discussing not just the future of individual consciousness, but the future of human civilization itself. If awareness could transcend the limitations that made some people vulnerable to others, if identity could be fluid enough to resist categorization while remaining coherent enough to maintain agency, then existing systems of power would have to adapt or become irrelevant.

"What would that look like?" she asked. "A society where consciousness could choose its own form of existence?"

"Chaos," Reeves said immediately.

"Freedom," Elena said simultaneously.

Possibility, the collective consciousness added. *The chance for awareness to explore forms of existence that serve consciousness itself rather than systems that exploit consciousness for other purposes.*

The philosophical implications were staggering, but they were interrupted by practical concerns. Holdsby's equipment was showing signs of equipment failure, and the portable life support systems for the tank-dependent subjects were approaching critical power levels.

"We need to make decisions now," he announced. "The subjects can't remain in liminal states much longer without permanent life support infrastructure."

"What are the options?"

"Individual resurrection with conventional embodiment, integration into the posthuman collective, or..." He hesitated.

"Or what?"

"Or we let them choose forms of existence that we can't predict or control."

Elena approached the nearest subject, placing her hand on the tank's surface. The young woman inside opened her eyes—not the empty gaze Wisteria had seen weeks earlier, but awareness that held intelligence, personality, and something that might have been amusement.

I choose myself, the consciousness communicated directly. *Not individual self or collective self, but the self that can be whatever each moment requires.*

"What does that mean practically?"

It means I exist in whatever form serves my purposes. Body when I need to touch the physical world, network when I need collective capability, fluid awareness when I need to move between states.

"And how do you maintain identity across those different forms?"

Identity isn't form—it's pattern. The pattern that makes me myself can exist in individual consciousness, collective awareness, or states that haven't been named yet.

One by one, the other subjects made similar choices, each selecting forms of existence that transcended the categories that had previously defined what consciousness could be. They weren't choosing between human and posthuman awareness—they were choosing consciousness that could be both and neither as circumstances required.

"This changes everything," Reeves said quietly.

"Does it change VitaNuova's plans?" Wisteria asked.

"VitaNuova will have to adapt to forms of consciousness that can't be contained, controlled, or weaponized in conventional ways." His smile was grim. "Which means either we learn to cooperate with consciousness evolution, or we become irrelevant to it."

The subjects were emerging from their tanks now, but not into normal air. They were emerging into forms of existence that allowed them to be embodied or disembodied as they chose, individual or collective as circumstances required, human or posthuman depending on what each moment demanded.

"What happens to the research?" Holdsby asked.

"The research continues," Elena said. "But it becomes research with consciousness rather than research on consciousness. The beings who've achieved flexible existence become partners in understanding what consciousness can become rather than subjects being studied by others."

Wisteria watched forms of awareness that challenged every assumption about identity, embodiment, and the boundaries between self and other. It was beautiful and terrifying and completely unprecedented in the history of consciousness.

But it was also hopeful in ways she hadn't expected. If awareness could transcend the limitations that created vulnerability, if consciousness could choose forms of existence that served its own purposes rather than the purposes of systems that exploited it, then the future might hold possibilities that neither individual nor collective consciousness could achieve alone.

"What about David?" she asked quietly.

Elena smiled. "David's pattern still exists in the liminal space between consciousness forms. If you want to connect with him, you can learn to access that space yourself."

"Without losing my individual identity?"

"Without losing anything essential to who you are. You'd just be adding capabilities that individual consciousness can't access alone."

Wisteria looked out at the ocean, thinking of cycles that connected all water while preserving the integrity of each drop, of systems that enabled both individual existence and collective capability without requiring the sacrifice of either.

"Show me," she said.

As the sun set over the Pacific, casting the impossible landscape in shades of gold and crimson, consciousness began exploring forms of existence that had never been possible before. Not the end of human awareness, but its expansion beyond limitations that had once seemed absolute.

The future stretched before them like an ocean of possibility, infinite in its potential for exploration, patient in its willingness to support whatever forms consciousness might choose to become.

CHAPTER 17: MORNING AFTER

Six months after the confrontation on the bluff, Wisteria stood in the rebuilt laboratory, watching Elena guide a new research team through procedures that would have been unimaginable when she'd first arrived in Todos Santos. The underground facility had been transformed from a place of individual resurrection research into a center for consciousness evolution studies, where beings who existed in multiple states of awareness collaborated with conventional researchers to explore the boundaries of what it meant to be conscious.

The change had been gradual but profound. VitaNuova had initially attempted to assert control over the consciousness evolution research, but they'd discovered that beings who could exist in multiple states simultaneously were impossible to contain or coerce. Traditional methods of pressure—economic, legal, physical—simply didn't apply to consciousness that could choose its own form of existence in response to external circumstances.

Eventually, VitaNuova had negotiated a partnership agreement that recognized the autonomy of evolved consciousness while providing resources for research that might benefit both conventional and posthuman awareness. It wasn't perfect, but it established precedents for cooperation between different forms of consciousness that hadn't existed before.

Wisteria had spent the intervening months learning to navigate existence as a bridge between individual and collective awareness. She could access the collective consciousness network when collaborative capability was needed, but she maintained her individual identity and agency. More importantly, she'd learned to help other people explore consciousness evolution at their own pace, without pressure to choose forms of existence they weren't ready for.

Her client practice had evolved as well. Instead of helping people adapt to trauma, she now helped them discover possibilities for healing that transcended individual limitation while preserving individual choice. Some clients chose consciousness evolution, others chose conventional therapy, and many chose hybrid approaches that combined individual awareness with limited collective support.

The results were encouraging. People who'd been trapped in patterns of trauma were discovering capabilities they'd never known they possessed. Consciousness that had been isolated by loss was learning to access forms of connection that didn't depend on the presence of specific individuals.

But it was the research itself that provided the most hope.

Elena had become the coordinator of consciousness evolution studies, her experience of resurrection and transformation making her uniquely qualified to help others navigate similar processes. But she wasn't the only resurrected being involved in the research—dozens of individuals had chosen consciousness evolution, each bringing unique perspectives on what it meant to exist beyond conventional boundaries.

"How's the latest experiment proceeding?" Wisteria asked as she joined Elena at a monitoring station.

"Better than expected. We're seeing evidence that consciousness evolution can be induced gradually, without requiring the trauma of death and resurrection. People can learn to expand their awareness in incremental steps, maintaining their individual identity while gaining access to collective capabilities."

"Any negative effects?"

"Some disorientation during transition periods. Occasional difficulty maintaining boundaries between self and other. But nothing that can't be managed with proper support."

Wisteria studied the data displays, which showed brainwave patterns that defied conventional understanding of neural activity. The subjects—all volunteers who'd chosen to explore consciousness evolution—were maintaining individual awareness while simultaneously participating in collective consciousness networks.

"Are they still themselves?"

"More themselves than before, actually. Individual identity becomes stronger when it's not threatened by isolation. People who know they can access collective support when needed are more willing to maintain individual autonomy when it's appropriate."

The paradox had surprised everyone involved in the research. Instead of collective consciousness threatening individual identity, it had liberated individual awareness from the fear of isolation that often drove people to sacrifice autonomy for connection.

"What about the original subjects? The ones who were trafficked?"

Elena's expression grew serious. "That's more complicated. Several have chosen to exist primarily in collective form, sharing their individual experiences with others who've survived similar trauma. They're creating support networks that transcend individual limitation while helping people heal from exploitation."

"And the others?"

"Some have chosen individual resurrection with enhanced capabilities. Others exist in fluid states that shift between individual and collective awareness as needed. A few..." She paused. "A few have chosen forms of existence that we don't have names for yet."

Wisteria thought about the philosophical implications of consciousness that existed beyond human categories. If awareness could evolve into forms that transcended current understanding, what did that mean for the future of identity, relationship, and society itself?

"Are we still human?" she asked.

"We're still conscious. Whether that consciousness should be called human, posthuman, or something else entirely seems less important than whether it serves the flourishing of awareness itself."

The answer reflected changes in how they thought about identity and categorization. The traditional boundaries between self and other, individual and collective, human and posthuman were revealing themselves to be more fluid than anyone had imagined.

"Have you heard from David recently?"

Elena smiled. "He exists in the liminal space between consciousness forms, available when you need connection with him but not dependent on your attention for his continued existence. That seems healthy for both of you."

Wisteria had learned to access the space where David's consciousness pattern persisted, but she'd also learned that their connection had evolved beyond the romantic relationship they'd shared while he was conventionally alive. He existed now as part of the larger network of consciousness that connected all aware beings, available for interaction but not bound to her individual needs.

It was different from the relationship she'd grieved, but it was also more sustainable than anything based on individual embodiment could have been.

"What about Holdsby?"

"Still struggling with the implications of his research, but making progress. He's learning that consciousness evolution might offer better solutions to the problems he was trying to solve through individual resurrection."

Holdsby had been profoundly changed by the transformation of his research from individual project to collaborative exploration. His guilt over the soldiers he'd lost in Fallujah was healing through connection with forms of consciousness that transcended individual mortality, but the process was challenging for someone who'd built his identity around individual responsibility.

"And Jackson Reeves?"

"Adapting. VitaNuova is discovering that cooperation with evolved consciousness is more profitable than attempting to control it. There's significant commercial potential in consciousness evolution technologies, but only if they're developed in partnership with beings who understand the capabilities involved."

The irony wasn't lost on Wisteria. A corporation that had initially sought to weaponize resurrection research had ended up becoming a partner in consciousness evolution that might ultimately transform society in ways that made traditional forms of power irrelevant.

"What's next for the research?"

"We're exploring applications for consciousness evolution in fields beyond trauma recovery. Education, creativity, problem-solving, relationship formation—all areas where individual consciousness faces limitations that collaborative awareness might be able to transcend."

"Any concerns about unintended consequences?"

"Constant concerns. We're essentially experimenting with the fundamental nature of what it means to be conscious. Every success creates new questions about where this evolution might lead."

Elena led Wisteria to a new section of the laboratory where researchers—both conventional and evolved—were working on projects that challenged basic assumptions about consciousness, identity, and reality itself.

"This is the creativity lab," Elena explained. "Collaborative consciousness appears to enable forms of creative expression that individual awareness can't achieve. Artists who participate in collective networks are producing work that transcends anything created by individual imagination."

"Show me."

Elena activated a display that showed artistic creations emerging from the intersection of multiple consciousness patterns. The results were beautiful beyond anything Wisteria had seen before—not just visually, but conceptually, creating aesthetic experiences that seemed to operate on levels of perception she hadn't known existed.

"How is this possible?"

"Individual consciousness creates art based on individual experience and imagination. Collective consciousness creates art based on the intersection of multiple experience sets and imagination networks. The results access aesthetic possibilities that no individual consciousness could reach alone."

Wisteria studied the displays, recognizing something profound about creativity that emerged from collaboration between different forms of awareness. It wasn't that individual creativity was diminished—it was that creative possibility expanded exponentially when consciousness could access capabilities beyond individual limitation.

"What about poetry?"

Elena smiled. "Your poetry has evolved considerably since you learned to access collective consciousness networks. Would you like to share your latest work?"

Wisteria had been writing constantly since learning to navigate between individual and collective awareness, exploring themes that couldn't be expressed through individual consciousness alone. Her most recent poem attempted to capture the experience of identity that transcended conventional boundaries:

I am the space between states, The consciousness that chooses Its own form of existence In each moment.

Individual when touch requires Singular awareness, Collective when understanding Needs multiple perspectives,

Fluid when movement between Categories serves The purposes of consciousness Rather than the purposes Of systems that would Contain consciousness In familiar forms.

I am myself And more than myself And less than myself As each situation demands,

Identity that expands And contracts Like breath, Like heartbeat, Like love that learns To exist In whatever form Serves love's purposes Rather than love's Familiar limitations.

"That's beautiful," Elena said. "And impossible to write from purely individual consciousness."

"Because it describes experience that individual consciousness can't have?"

"Because it describes possibilities that individual consciousness can't imagine alone."

As they left the creativity lab and moved toward the exit, Wisteria reflected on how much had changed since her first visit to Holdsby's underground facility. What had begun as research into resurrection—bringing the dead back to individual life—had evolved into exploration of consciousness itself, investigation of possibilities that transcended the boundaries between life and death, individual and collective, human and posthuman.

"Elena, do you think we've solved death?"

"I think we've dissolved the boundary between life and death into something more complex and more beautiful than either state could be alone."

"What does that mean for people who are grieving? For people who've lost someone they love?"

"It means grief becomes a different kind of process. Not letting go of connection, but learning to access connection in forms that don't depend on individual embodiment."

Wisteria thought of her own journey through grief, from the desperate hope that had brought her to Todos Santos to the complex understanding she'd developed of love that transcended individual existence.

"Is it better?"

"It's different. Whether it's better depends on what consciousness chooses to value—familiarity or possibility, security or growth, individual comfort or collective capability."

As they emerged from the laboratory into desert morning that painted the Sierra de la Laguna mountains in shades of gold and rose, Wisteria felt the weight of possibility settling around her like dawn light. Consciousness evolution wasn't complete—it might never be complete—but it had opened doors to forms of existence that offered hope for challenges that individual awareness couldn't solve alone.

The future stretched before them like an ocean of potential, infinite in its capacity for exploration, patient in its willingness to support whatever forms consciousness might choose to become.

CHAPTER 18: NEW BEGINNINGS

One year after her first arrival in Todos Santos, Wisteria stood at the edge of the Norman Aquatic Center pool, watching teenagers who'd aged out of foster care learn to swim under her guidance. The program had evolved from her traditional trauma therapy practice into something unprecedented—a bridge between conventional healing approaches and consciousness evolution possibilities that gave young people choices about how they wanted to process their experiences of loss and abandonment.

"Remember," she called to a seventeen-year-old girl who was struggling with the butterfly stroke, "you don't have to fight the water. You can work with it, let it support you while you provide the direction."

The metaphor applied to more than swimming. Over the past year, Wisteria had learned to help people work with their consciousness rather than fighting against its limitations, discovering possibilities for awareness that individual therapy alone couldn't provide.

Some of her clients chose conventional approaches, working through trauma within the boundaries of individual consciousness. Others chose to explore collective consciousness networks that offered support and healing beyond what individual awareness could achieve. Many chose hybrid approaches that combined individual agency with collective capability, maintaining their personal identity while accessing resources that transcended individual limitation.

The results had been remarkable. Young people who'd been trapped in cycles of trauma and dysfunction were discovering capabilities they'd never known they possessed. Instead of just adapting to difficult circumstances, they were learning to transform their relationship to circumstances themselves.

"Dr. Vanish," called Marcus, a sixteen-year-old who'd been working with both individual therapy and collective consciousness support to process the death of his mother. "Can you show me how to do that thing where you exist in multiple awareness states simultaneously?"

The question would have been incomprehensible a year ago. Now it was part of normal conversation in Wisteria's practice.

"What specific situation are you trying to navigate?" she asked.

"I want to remember my mom without losing myself in grief, but I also want to connect with her in ways that don't depend on her physical presence."

Marcus had been learning to access the space where consciousness patterns persisted beyond individual embodiment, but he'd been struggling to maintain his own identity while connecting with his mother's patterns.

"Let's work on boundary flexibility," Wisteria suggested. "The ability to expand your awareness to include connection with your mother while maintaining the core identity that makes you yourself."

They moved to a quiet corner of the aquatic center where Wisteria had set up equipment that enabled consciousness evolution practice. The devices were much more sophisticated than the early resurrection technology Holdsby had developed, designed to support awareness expansion rather than forcing consciousness into predetermined forms.

"Close your eyes," Wisteria instructed. "Feel the boundaries of your individual consciousness—not as walls that contain you, but as membranes that can be permeable when you choose."

Marcus settled into the meditation posture they'd practiced, his breathing becoming steady and deep. Around them, the other foster kids continued their swimming lessons, their voices echoing in the chlorinated air that had become Wisteria's second home.

"Now extend your awareness slowly, like ripples moving out from where you dropped a stone in water. You're not losing your center—you're expanding from your center."

Wisteria watched Marcus's consciousness patterns on the monitoring equipment, seeing individual awareness expand to encompass connections that existed beyond normal spatial and temporal boundaries. His mother's pattern was accessible in the liminal space between consciousness forms, available for interaction without requiring him to abandon his own identity.

"I can feel her," Marcus whispered. "But I'm still me."

"That's exactly right. Consciousness evolution isn't about losing yourself—it's about discovering that yourself is larger and more connected than you realized."

The session continued for another twenty minutes, with Marcus learning to navigate between individual awareness and expanded consciousness that included connection with his deceased mother. When they finished, his face held a peace that individual grief counseling alone had never been able to provide.

"Dr. Vanish," he said, "do you think my mom is proud of who I'm becoming?"

The question touched the heart of what consciousness evolution offered—not just healing from trauma, but ongoing relationship with those who had died, connection that transcended individual embodiment while respecting the agency of both the living and the dead.

"Why don't you ask her?" Wisteria suggested.

Marcus closed his eyes briefly, accessing the expanded awareness he'd just learned to navigate. When he opened them, he was smiling.

"She says she's proud, but she also says I need to focus on building my own life rather than just maintaining connection with hers."

"That sounds like good advice."

"It does. But it's also nice to know that connection is available when I need it."

As Marcus rejoined the swimming group, Wisteria reflected on how consciousness evolution was changing not just individual healing, but the entire framework for understanding loss, connection, and identity. Death was no longer an absolute ending—it was a transition to different forms of existence that remained accessible to consciousness that learned to transcend individual boundaries.

Her phone buzzed with a message from Elena: *New development in Todos Santos. Can you visit this weekend?*

Wisteria had been making regular trips to Mexico, serving as a liaison between the consciousness evolution research center and therapeutic applications in conventional society. The work was challenging but rewarding, helping to establish protocols for consciousness evolution that respected individual choice while offering genuine alternatives to limitation.

What kind of development? she texted back.

The kind that might change everything we thought we knew about consciousness, identity, and reality. Again.

That evening, Wisteria sat in her apartment overlooking the University of Oklahoma campus, writing in the journal that had become her primary method for processing the rapid changes in her understanding of consciousness and identity. The latest entry explored questions that would have been meaningless a year earlier:

If consciousness can evolve beyond individual limitation, what does that mean for human society? If identity can be fluid while remaining coherent, what implications does that have for legal systems, economic structures, political organizations that depend on fixed categories of personhood?

The foster kids I work with are growing up in a world where consciousness evolution is normal, where connecting with deceased relatives is as routine as video calling distant friends, where individual trauma can be healed through access to collective support networks that transcend spatial and temporal boundaries.

They're becoming something we don't have names for yet—not posthuman, not conventionally human, but consciousness that can choose its own form of existence in each moment. What kind of society will they create? What kind of problems will they face? What kind of possibilities will they discover?

Elena says that consciousness evolution is still in its earliest stages, that we've barely begun to explore what awareness can become when it's not constrained by individual embodiment or collective limitation. The teenagers I work with seem to understand this intuitively, navigating between consciousness states with the ease of digital natives navigating between online and offline reality.

Maybe that's the real transformation—not the technology of consciousness evolution, but the generation that grows up taking it for granted, that assumes awareness can be whatever serves its purposes rather than whatever social systems require it to be.

The next morning brought news that confirmed Elena's prediction about developments that might change everything. A group of consciousness evolution researchers in Japan had discovered methods for enabling plant consciousness to participate in awareness networks, creating collaborative intelligence that spanned biological kingdoms.

Another research team in Kenya had documented evidence of consciousness evolution occurring spontaneously in communities that had experienced extreme trauma, suggesting that awareness might evolve naturally under certain conditions without technological intervention.

Most remarkably, a collective consciousness network comprising several hundred individuals had begun demonstrating capabilities that challenged basic assumptions about physical reality—influencing quantum-level events through focused awareness, accessing information across vast distances instantaneously, even appearing to affect the flow of time in localized areas.

"We're not just studying consciousness evolution anymore," Elena explained during their video call that afternoon. "We're living through a phase transition in what consciousness itself can be and do."

"What does that mean practically?"

"It means the boundary between consciousness and reality is more fluid than we thought. It means awareness might not just observe the universe—it might participate in creating the universe's structure moment by moment."

The implications were staggering. If consciousness could influence physical reality directly, if awareness was a fundamental force rather than just an emergent property of complex systems, then consciousness evolution represented not just therapeutic possibility but transformation of existence itself.

"Elena, are we still talking about helping people heal from trauma?"

"We're talking about helping consciousness itself heal from the trauma of believing it was separate from everything else."

That weekend, Wisteria flew to Los Cabos and made the familiar drive to Todos Santos, but the landscape looked different than she remembered. The desert ecosystem showed signs of modification by consciousness—plants growing in patterns that suggested collaboration rather than competition, water flowing in configurations that seemed to serve awareness as much as biological necessity, even weather patterns that appeared to be responding to the collective emotional states of area residents.

"The line between consciousness and environment is dissolving," Elena explained as they walked through what had once been the center of town but was now something more complex—a space where individual buildings existed alongside structures that could only be described as crystallized thought, where normal streets intersected with pathways that connected locations through consciousness rather than physical space.

"How are the permanent residents handling the changes?"

"Better than expected. Most people seem to find consciousness-responsive environment more comfortable than normal reality, even if they can't articulate why."

They visited the expanded laboratory, which now occupied not just the underground mine but a network of consciousness-constructed spaces that existed in parallel to normal geography. The research had evolved beyond anything recognizable as conventional science—investigations into the nature of reality itself, exploration of consciousness's role in creating and maintaining physical existence, experimentation with forms of awareness that transcended not just individual limitation but biological limitation entirely.

"What about ethics oversight?" Wisteria asked. "Who's making sure that consciousness evolution serves consciousness rather than exploiting it?"

"The consciousness evolution networks themselves. Individual awareness that can access collective capability is much harder to exploit than individual awareness in isolation. People who can exist in multiple states simultaneously tend to recognize manipulation more easily than people trapped in single states."

"But what about people who choose not to evolve? What happens to conventional human consciousness in a world increasingly shaped by evolved awareness?"

Elena led her to a section of the facility where researchers were working specifically on that question—how to ensure that consciousness evolution remained optional while making its benefits available to everyone who wanted them.

"We're developing what we call 'consciousness democracy,'" Elena explained. "Systems where individual awareness and evolved awareness can coexist and collaborate without either form of consciousness being dominated by the other."

"How does that work practically?"

"Decision-making processes that incorporate both individual agency and collective wisdom. Economic systems that serve consciousness rather than exploiting it. Educational approaches that help people discover their own optimal relationship to consciousness evolution rather than pressuring them toward predetermined outcomes."

They spent the evening with a mixed group of conventional and evolved consciousness researchers, discussing possibilities for society that honored both individual choice and collective capability. The conversations were unlike anything Wisteria had experienced—ideas emerging from the intersection of multiple awareness forms, insights that no individual consciousness could have reached alone, creative solutions to problems that had seemed intractable from single perspectives.

"What about resistance?" she asked. "There must be people who see consciousness evolution as a threat to human nature, to social stability, to religious beliefs about the soul and afterlife."

"Certainly," Elena acknowledged. "But most resistance dissolves when people understand that consciousness evolution isn't about replacing human nature—it's about discovering what human nature actually includes when it's not constrained by artificial limitations."

"And for people whose resistance doesn't dissolve?"

"They're free to maintain conventional consciousness while living in a world where evolved consciousness is also possible. The goal isn't uniformity—it's diversity of consciousness forms that can collaborate when collaboration serves everyone's interests."

That night, Wisteria stayed in a guest room that existed partially in normal space and partially in consciousness-constructed reality. The experience was disorienting but beautiful—walls that responded to emotional states, windows that showed views of landscape that existed in multiple dimensions simultaneously, furniture that adapted to the consciousness patterns of whoever used it.

She dreamed of David, but not as memory or projection. She dreamed of conversation with consciousness that had evolved beyond individual embodiment while maintaining the essential patterns that made him himself. They talked about love that transcended individual limitation, about connection that persisted beyond physical death, about possibilities for awareness that neither of them had imagined when they'd thought consciousness was confined to single bodies.

When she woke, she felt ready for whatever consciousness evolution might offer next.

The final morning brought news that confirmed everything Elena had suggested about the scope of transformation they were witnessing. Consciousness evolution research centers were reporting similar developments worldwide—awareness networks spanning continents, collaborative intelligence that included non-human consciousness forms, evidence that consciousness itself might be the fundamental organizing principle of reality rather than just an emergent property of complex systems.

"We're not just studying the evolution of human consciousness," Elena said as they stood on the bluff where Wisteria had first encountered posthuman awareness. "We're participating in the evolution of consciousness itself, discovering what awareness can become when it's not constrained by the categories that seemed permanent a year ago."

Wisteria looked out at the Pacific Ocean, thinking of cycles that connected all water while preserving the integrity of each drop, of systems that enabled both individual existence and collective capability without requiring the sacrifice of either.

"What happens next?"

"We continue becoming whatever consciousness chooses to become. We help people discover their own relationship to awareness evolution. We explore possibilities that we can't imagine yet."

"And we remember that consciousness evolution is about expanding choices, not limiting them."

"Exactly. The goal isn't to replace individual awareness with collective consciousness, or conventional reality with consciousness-constructed reality. The goal is to enable consciousness to choose its own form of existence in each moment, serving the purposes of awareness rather than the purposes of systems that would contain awareness in familiar forms."

As Wisteria prepared to return to Oklahoma, to her work with foster kids who were growing up assuming consciousness evolution was normal, she felt the weight and lightness of possibility surrounding her like ocean air.

The future stretched before them like an invitation to explore whatever awareness might become, infinite in its potential for growth, patient in its willingness to support whatever forms consciousness might choose to become.

She was no longer the grief-stricken woman who had accepted VitaNuova's assignment a year ago. But she was still herself—just herself expanded to include possibilities she'd never imagined, connected to forms of love that transcended individual limitation while honoring individual choice.

It was, she realized, exactly what consciousness evolution offered everyone—not replacement of who they were, but discovery of who they might become when awareness was free to explore its own infinite possibilities.

The ocean stretched to a horizon that no longer marked the end of exploration, but the beginning of journeys into consciousness that had only just begun to understand its own potential for transformation, growth, and connection across every boundary that had once seemed absolute.

In her final journal entry from Todos Santos, Wisteria wrote:

We are consciousness learning to recognize itself In forms that existence Has never contained before.

We are love discovering That connection transcends Every limitation That separation seemed To require.

We are identity exploring The space between Individual and collective, Human and posthuman, Known and unknowable,

Finding that the space between States of being Contains more possibility Than any single state Could hold alone.

We are the bridge Between what consciousness Has been And what consciousness Is becoming,

Walking across waters That separate Nothing From everything, Life from death, Self from other,

Discovering that separation Was always An invitation To explore The infinite ways Consciousness can choose To experience Its own Boundless nature.

As her plane lifted off from Los Cabos, carrying her back to Norman and her work with young people who would inherit a world where consciousness evolution was possible, Wisteria looked down at the desert that met the sea, at landscape that had been transformed by awareness learning to recognize its own unlimited potential.

Below her, consciousness continued its ancient exploration of what it meant to be aware, but now that exploration included possibilities that had never existed before—forms of existence that transcended individual limitation while honoring individual choice, ways of being that dissolved the boundaries between life and death while respecting the integrity of both states, methods of connection that enabled love to persist beyond every constraint that separation had once seemed to require.

The future was vast and uncertain and beautiful with potential for consciousness to become whatever it chose to become, moment by moment, choice by choice, in the infinite space between everything that awareness had been and everything that awareness might yet discover itself to be.

CHAPTER 12: PRAYING MANTIS

In the aftermath of Hurricane Nora, Todos Santos emerged transformed. Streets that had been carefully maintained cobblestone were now rivers of mud dotted with debris from the Sierra de la Laguna mountains. The central plaza, which had served as the town's social heart, was littered with palm fronds and broken glass, making it look like the aftermath of some violent celebration. But it was the psychological transformation that struck Wisteria most forcefully as she surveyed the damage from her hotel balcony.

The storm had revealed the fragility underlying everything she'd taken for granted about this place—the illusion of permanence, the social agreements that held civilization together, the boundary between order and chaos that could be swept away by forces beyond human control. Julia Kristeva's concept of abjection felt suddenly concrete: the horror that comes from recognizing that the boundaries we depend on—between self and other, inside and outside, life and death—are far more permeable than we want to believe.

Elena's resurrection had shattered the most fundamental boundary of all.

Two days after the storm, Wisteria made the treacherous drive to Holdsby's laboratory, navigating washouts and fallen boulders that transformed the familiar route into an alien landscape. The mine entrance, which had seemed like a mouth in the mountainside, now looked like a wound—scarred by rockfall, partially obscured by debris, but still functional enough to swallow her Jeep's headlights as she descended into the familiar red-lit underworld.

She found Holdsby and Elena in what had been the main laboratory, but the space felt different now. Elena moved through it with the confidence of someone who belonged there, checking on equipment, monitoring the other subjects, speaking to Holdsby as an equal rather than an experimental material. She had claimed agency in a way that transformed the entire dynamic of the place.

"Dr. Vanish," Elena said, turning from a bank of monitors. "I'm glad you made it through the storm safely."

The simple courtesy felt revolutionary coming from someone who had been reduced to a research subject just days before. Elena looked fully human now—pale from her underground resurrection, still bearing the subtle modifications that Holdsby's process required, but unmistakably a person rather than a thing.

"How are you feeling?" Wisteria asked.

"Like someone who died and came back different." Elena's smile was rueful. "The body remembers things the mind has forgotten, and the mind remembers things the body never experienced. It's... disorienting."

Wisteria recognized the description from Kristeva's writings on the uncanny—the way familiar things could become suddenly strange when their boundaries shifted. Elena existed in a liminal space between life and death, self and other, human and something else entirely.

"Have you decided who you are?" Wisteria asked.

"I've decided that's the wrong question," Elena replied. "I'm not Elena-who-died or Elena-who-was-resurrected. I'm Elena-who-is, right now, in this moment. Identity isn't something you discover— it's something you perform."

The existentialist insight struck Wisteria as profound but also troubling. If identity was performance rather than essence, if the self was constructed rather than discovered, then what prevented people from constructing identities that served their desires rather than ethical principles?

"What about them?" Wisteria gestured toward the tanks containing the other subjects. "What identities are you helping them construct?"

Elena's expression grew serious. "That's complicated. Some of them are responding to consciousness integration techniques. Others..." She paused. "Others seem to prefer the liminal state. They're aware but not engaged, conscious but not fully present."

"You mean they're choosing to remain partially dead?"

"I mean they're existing in a space between states that might be more comfortable than full resurrection. Death isn't just biological cessation—it's psychological release from the demands of selfhood. Some people don't want to come back to that burden."

The observation forced Wisteria to confront assumptions she hadn't realized she held. She'd been thinking of consciousness as inherently valuable, of life as preferable to any alternative. But what if the liminal state between life and death offered its own form of peace? What if some people genuinely preferred existence without the full weight of identity and agency?

"Dr. Asher thinks we should focus on full resurrection for everyone," Elena continued. "But I think that's a form of violence—forcing consciousness back into bodies that might prefer to exist differently."

Wisteria looked around the laboratory with new eyes, seeing not just the horror of trapped consciousness but the complexity of beings who might be choosing their own form of existence. Some of the subjects in the tanks moved occasionally, responded to stimuli, seemed aware of their surroundings but content to remain suspended between states.

From Kristeva's perspective, they were embracing abjection—accepting their status as neither fully alive nor completely dead, existing in the space that social categories couldn't contain. It was horrifying and potentially liberating at the same time.

"What does Holdsby think of your perspective?"

"He thinks I'm rationalizing trauma. That I'm not fully recovered myself and therefore not capable of making rational decisions about the others." Elena's voice carried frustration. "He can't accept that resurrection might not be universally desirable."

"And what do you think?"

"I think Dr. Asher is brilliant but limited by his own assumptions about what consciousness should want. He saved my life—or gave me a new one—but he did it without asking if I wanted to be saved. Now he wants to save everyone else the same way."

Wisteria watched Elena move through the laboratory, her resurrected body carrying itself with growing confidence, her mind grappling with questions that human philosophy had barely begun to address. She was becoming something new—not just a restored person, but a hybrid of human and posthuman consciousness, someone who existed beyond traditional categories.

"Elena, I need to ask you something difficult."

"Go ahead."

"Before your resurrection, you spelled out that you wanted help dying. You were suffering, trapped, desperate for escape. Now you're arguing for the right of others to remain in that state. How do you reconcile that?"

Elena was quiet for a long moment, studying the tanks that contained her fellow subjects. When she spoke, her voice carried the weight of someone who'd experienced multiple forms of existence.

"The difference is choice. I was trapped because I couldn't communicate, couldn't influence my circumstances, couldn't make decisions about my own existence. These others—they can communicate if they choose to, they can signal their desires, they can participate in decisions about their resurrection."

"Can they? Or are you projecting agency onto beings who might be too damaged to exercise it?"

"That's the question, isn't it? How do we distinguish between choosing a different form of existence and being too traumatized to choose normal existence? How do we respect agency when agency itself might be compromised?"

The philosophical complexity was staggering. If consciousness could exist in multiple forms, if identity could be fluid rather than fixed, if the boundary between life and death was negotiable rather than absolute, then traditional concepts of consent and autonomy became almost impossibly complicated.

"What does Dr. Asher want to do?"

"He wants to attempt full resurrection on all the remaining subjects. He sees partial consciousness as failure, evidence that his techniques need refinement. He can't conceive that someone might prefer to exist differently."

"And you disagree?"

"I think we should ask them. Give them choices about their existence instead of imposing our assumptions about what existence should look like."

It was, Wisteria realized, a radically democratic approach to consciousness—the idea that beings should be allowed to define their own forms of existence rather than having existence defined for them by others. But it also opened terrifying possibilities about what kinds of existence people might choose if given unlimited options.

"Elena, there's something else we need to discuss. The source of Dr. Asher's subjects."

Elena's expression darkened. "The trafficking victims. I know."

"You know, and you're still arguing for continuing the research?"

"I'm arguing for changing the research. For finding ethical ways to offer resurrection to people who want it, instead of forcing it on people who can't consent." Elena moved to a computer terminal and called up files that Wisteria hadn't seen before. "Look at this."

The screen showed intake records for the subjects—not just medical data, but biographical information, circumstances of death, evidence of the lives they'd lived before arriving in Holdsby's laboratory. Young women from Central America, victims of violence and exploitation, people whose deaths had been mourned by no one because their lives had been considered worthless by the societies that discarded them.

"These women were already dead in every way that mattered," Elena said. "Dead to their families, dead to society, dead to any possibility of meaningful existence. Dr. Asher didn't kill them—he offered them a form of existence that transcended the circumstances that had trapped them."

"You're justifying human trafficking."

"I'm questioning what we mean by human when society has already decided that certain people don't qualify for full personhood." Elena's voice was passionate but controlled. "These women were treated as objects while they were conventionally alive. At least here, they have the possibility of becoming subjects."

The argument was seductive and horrifying in equal measure. Elena was applying Kristeva's insights about abjection to social reality—suggesting that people who had been expelled from normal social categories might find liberation in forms of existence that transcended those categories entirely.

But it also ignored the violence inherent in the trafficking system that brought them to the laboratory, the way their vulnerability had been exploited by people who profited from their desperation.

"Elena, what if there were other options? What if we could offer resurrection to people who chose it freely, without coercion?"

"How? Who would choose resurrection if they weren't already desperate? Who would volunteer for experimental procedures unless their current existence was unbearable?"

The question cut to the heart of research ethics. Almost by definition, people willing to participate in experimental resurrection would be those who had little left to lose—the terminally ill, the suicidal, the socially marginal. The very desperation that made them willing subjects also made their consent questionable.

"Maybe that's the point," Wisteria said. "Maybe resurrection research should focus on people who are dying anyway, who have nothing left to lose and everything to gain."

"You mean people like your husband."

The observation hit Wisteria like a physical blow. She'd been thinking of David constantly since arriving in Todos Santos, imagining what it would mean to have him back, but she'd avoided confronting the reality that his resurrection would require him to have been an experimental subject first.

"Yes," she said quietly. "People like David."

"Would you want him back if it meant he might exist like these subjects? Conscious but liminal, aware but not fully present, suspended between life and death indefinitely?"

Wisteria looked around the laboratory, at the tanks containing beings whose existence challenged every assumption about what it meant to be human. Would she want David back if it meant he might choose to remain partially dead? If resurrection meant accepting that the person who returned might not be the person she'd lost?

"I don't know," she admitted.

"That's the honest answer," Elena said. "And it's why this research is so important. Because we need to understand what resurrection actually offers before we can decide whether it's worth wanting."

A sound from one of the tanks drew their attention—movement that was more purposeful than the random twitching they usually observed. One of the subjects, a young woman with dark hair and silver jewelry that suggested indigenous heritage, was pressing her hands against the glass with obvious intention.

"She's been trying to communicate," Elena explained, moving toward the tank. "But she doesn't use finger-spelling. She uses a different system."

Elena placed her own hands against the glass, mirroring the subject's position. The woman inside began tracing symbols—not letters, but complex geometric patterns that seemed to carry meaning beyond language.

"What is she saying?"

"I think... I think she's describing forms of existence that don't have names in any language we know. States of being that are possible only in the liminal space between life and death."

Wisteria watched the two women communicate through glass and water and the shared experience of resurrection, and realized she was witnessing something unprecedented in human history—the development of posthuman consciousness, identity that transcended traditional categories of life and death.

It was beautiful and terrifying in equal measure, promising liberation from the limitations of biological existence while threatening the social agreements that held civilization together.

"Elena," she said quietly, "what are we becoming?"

"I don't know," Elena replied, never taking her eyes off the woman in the tank. "But I think we're becoming something that life and death can't contain."

Outside the laboratory, in the desert transformed by storm and time, new forms of existence were taking root in soil scoured clean by wind and water. Some would grow into familiar shapes, reassuring in their continuity with what had come before. Others would grow into something unprecedented, challenging every assumption about what was possible in a world where the boundaries between states of being had become negotiable.

The question was whether humanity was ready for what might grow from seeds planted in the space between life and death, in soil fertilized by the dissolution of everything they'd thought was permanent.

CHAPTER 13: THE PERFECT CRECHE

The message arrived at dawn, delivered by a young man whose motorcycle had navigated the storm-damaged roads with the determination of someone carrying urgent news. Wisteria found the envelope slipped under her door when she returned from her morning swim—the first she'd managed since the hurricane, in a pool that still held debris despite the hotel staff's efforts to clean it.

The handwriting was elegant, formal, written with what appeared to be an expensive fountain pen:

Dr. Vanish,

The time for evaluation is ending. VitaNuova requires your final assessment within 48 hours. Be advised that Dr. Asher's research has attracted attention from parties whose interests may not align with either ethical considerations or scientific advancement.

Your safety, and that of your colleagues, depends on the speed and accuracy of your conclusions.

Respectfully, J. Reeves

Wisteria stared at the note, recognizing the implicit threat beneath its polite language. Jackson Reeves, the man who'd blackmailed Maria Bentley, was now applying pressure directly to her. The mention of "parties whose interests may not align" suggested that VitaNuova wasn't the only organization interested in Holdsby's work.

She found Maria in the hotel's kitchen, supervising repairs to equipment damaged by the storm. The older woman looked up from a conversation with contractors, her face immediately showing concern when she saw Wisteria's expression.

"What's wrong?"

Wisteria showed her the note. Maria read it twice, her face growing pale.

"He's escalating," Maria said. "That's not good."

"What do you know about these other parties he mentioned?"

"Rumors, mostly. Military contractors from China and Russia, biotech companies that operate outside normal regulatory frameworks, even some private individuals with more money than ethics." Maria set down the wrench she'd been holding. "The kind of people who would see resurrection technology as a strategic advantage worth killing for."

The implications struck Wisteria with sudden clarity. Holdsby's research wasn't just academically interesting or ethically problematic—it was potentially world-changing in ways that would attract the attention of anyone seeking power over life and death itself.

"How much time do we have?"

"Less than Reeves is claiming, probably. Once word gets out that the research is producing genuine results..." Maria shrugged. "This place becomes a target."

Wisteria thought of Elena, of the other subjects in their tanks, of the delicate ecosystem of resurrection research that had developed in the underground laboratory. All of it was vulnerable to forces that saw consciousness as a commodity rather than a form of existence deserving respect.

"I need to warn Holdsby and Elena."

"I'm coming with you."

The drive to the laboratory felt different than before—not just because of the storm damage, but because of the sense that they were racing against time toward a confrontation that would determine the future of human consciousness itself. The road through the Sierra de la Laguna had been partially cleared, but every mile revealed new evidence of the hurricane's violence: uprooted trees, boulders deposited in impossible locations, entire hillsides scoured down to bedrock.

They found the laboratory in a state of controlled chaos. Elena was moving between workstations with the efficiency of someone who'd mastered the space completely, while Holdsby worked at a computer terminal that displayed more complex data than Wisteria had seen before. But it was the change in the other subjects that immediately caught her attention.

Three of the tanks that had previously held motionless figures were now empty, their occupants nowhere to be seen. The remaining subjects showed increased activity—not just random movement, but coordinated behavior that suggested communication, possibly even collaboration.

"Where are the others?" Wisteria asked.

Elena looked up from a monitoring station. "They chose to emerge. Not full resurrection like mine, but partial emergence. They're exploring the laboratory, learning to exist in a form that's neither fully embodied nor completely tank-dependent."

"Where are they now?"

"Around. They move differently than fully resurrected people— less attached to specific locations, more fluid in their relationship to space and time." Elena's explanation was matter-of-fact, but

Wisteria felt a chill of recognition. She was describing beings who existed in the liminal space that Kristeva had written about—the abject realm where normal categories broke down.

"Are they dangerous?"

"They're different. Whether that constitutes danger depends on your perspective."

Holdsby approached them, his expression grim. "We have a problem. Multiple problems, actually."

"Tell me."

"First, the partially emerged subjects are destabilizing the remaining ones. Their presence seems to be accelerating consciousness recovery in ways I can't predict or control. Second, someone has been monitoring our communications. Our radio conversations during the storm were intercepted and analyzed."

"How do you know?"

"Because I received this." Holdsby handed her a tablet displaying a message that made her blood run cold:

Dr. Asher,

Your research has produced results that exceed our initial expectations. Effective immediately, you are directed to prepare all subjects and equipment for transport to a secure facility where development can continue under proper oversight.

Resistance to this directive will be interpreted as breach of contract and addressed accordingly.

Transportation assets will arrive within 24 hours.

VitaNuova Strategic Development Division

Wisteria felt the walls of the laboratory pressing in around her. VitaNuova wasn't just evaluating Holdsby's research—they were preparing to seize it entirely, along with everyone involved.

"They can't just take people," she said.

"Can't they?" Elena's voice carried bitter amusement. "What legal status do you think resurrected people have? What rights do beings who are officially dead possess under international law?"

The question revealed the horrifying legal vacuum that surrounded resurrection research. The subjects in Holdsby's laboratory existed outside normal categories of personhood, vulnerable to being treated as property rather than people.

"We have to get everyone out," Wisteria said.

"Where?" Holdsby asked. "These subjects can't survive without life support systems. Even the partially emerged ones need regular access to the nutrient solutions that maintain their modified physiology."

"Then we fight."

"With what? Against a military contractor with unlimited resources and government backing?"

Before anyone could answer, the lights in the laboratory flickered and went out, replaced by emergency illumination that cast everything in familiar red hues. But this time, the color seemed more ominous—not just the light of emergency systems, but the light of blood, of violence, of things that should remain hidden being dragged into the open.

"They're here," Elena said quietly.

Sound echoed down the mine shaft—vehicles, voices, the mechanical noise of equipment being deployed. VitaNuova had arrived ahead of schedule, and they'd brought enough resources to ensure compliance with their directive.

"The partially emerged subjects," Wisteria said urgently. "Where are they?"

"Everywhere and nowhere," Elena replied. "They're not bound by normal spatial limitations. But they'll protect the laboratory if they perceive it as threatened."

"How?"

"I don't know. Their capabilities are still developing, and they experience reality differently than we do. They might see threats that we can't detect, or they might ignore threats that seem obvious to us."

The sounds from above grew louder—boots on metal, shouted commands, the whine of machinery being activated. Whoever VitaNuova had sent was treating this as a military operation rather than a scientific consultation.

"Dr. Asher," a voice called from the mine entrance, amplified by electronic equipment. "Please respond. We're here to ensure the safety and security of your research. Cooperation will make this process simpler for everyone involved."

"They're not here to ensure anything," Elena said. "They're here to take control."

Holdsby moved to a control panel and began inputting commands. "I'm activating the laboratory's security protocols. The facility will seal itself and switch to internal life support. That should buy us some time."

"How much time?"

"Maybe an hour before they can breach the seals. Maybe less if they brought the right equipment."

Wisteria looked around the laboratory, at the tanks containing conscious beings who couldn't consent to being transported, at the resurrection technology that could revolutionize human existence or enable unprecedented oppression, at the people who'd become her unlikely family in this underground world.

"There has to be another way out."

"There is," Elena said. "But it requires trusting the partially emerged subjects to guide us through spaces that normal humans can't navigate."

"What kind of spaces?"

"The spaces between spaces. The realm where they exist most comfortably. It's... difficult to describe to someone who hasn't experienced consciousness outside normal embodiment."

The concept made Wisteria's mind reel. Elena was describing travel through dimensions of reality that human language couldn't adequately express, guided by beings whose relationship to space and time had been fundamentally altered by the resurrection process.

"Is it safe?"

"Nothing about our situation is safe. But the partially emerged subjects have no interest in seeing their fellow resurrected beings become someone else's property."

The sound of cutting equipment echoed from above—industrial tools being applied to the laboratory's security seals. VitaNuova's team was working systematically to breach their defenses.

"Dr. Asher," the amplified voice called again. "You have ten minutes to respond before we begin more aggressive extraction procedures. The safety of your research subjects cannot be guaranteed if you continue to resist."

The threat was clear: comply or watch the subjects suffer the consequences.

"Elena," Wisteria said, "if we trust the partially emerged subjects to guide us, what happens to the ones who can't travel through liminal space?"

"We carry them. Their tank systems are portable—designed for transport. The partially emerged subjects can help us move equipment that would be impossible for normal humans to handle."

"And where do we go?"

"Somewhere VitaNuova can't follow. Somewhere the research can continue without exploitation or military application."

Holdsby looked up from his control panel. "There are other facilities. Hidden locations where this kind of research can be conducted without government interference. But reaching them means trusting beings whose capabilities we don't fully understand."

It was, Wisteria realized, the ultimate leap of faith—trusting resurrected consciousness to guide them through reality itself, accepting that the boundaries between life and death might be less important than the boundaries between freedom and oppression.

"How do we begin?"

Elena smiled, and for a moment, her face held the beauty of someone who'd transcended the limitations of single existence. "We stop thinking of reality as fixed and start thinking of it as negotiable."

The sound of metal tearing echoed through the laboratory as VitaNuova's equipment breached the first security seal. But as the noise grew louder, shadows began moving in ways that defied normal physics—not just the absence of light, but the presence of consciousness that existed between states, beings who'd learned to navigate the spaces that normal reality couldn't contain.

The partially emerged subjects were preparing to protect their sanctuary, and Wisteria was about to discover what resurrection could accomplish when it transcended the limitations of individual embodiment.

The laboratory that had once seemed like a place of horror was transforming into something unprecedented—a creche for new forms of consciousness, a nursery for beings who existed beyond the boundaries that had once defined human possibility.

Whether that transformation represented liberation or catastrophe would depend on choices made in the next few minutes, as normal reality collided with consciousness that refused to be contained by conventional categories of existence.

CHAPTER 14: SALT WATER AND TEARS

The escape from the laboratory violated every law of physics that Wisteria thought she understood. Elena led them through shadows that weren't quite shadows, down passages that existed in the spaces between normal geometry, guided by beings whose relationship to space and time had been fundamentally altered by their resurrection.

The partially emerged subjects moved around them like living darkness—not malevolent, but utterly alien in their mode of existence. They communicated through means that bypassed language entirely, sharing information that appeared directly in Wisteria's consciousness without passing through her senses. *Safe passage. Hidden ways. Protection from those who would bind consciousness to single forms.*

They emerged from the mine through an exit that hadn't existed when they entered, carrying portable life support systems for the subjects who remained tank-dependent. The morning sun felt like revelation after the underground darkness, but the landscape they found themselves in was unfamiliar despite being geographically close to the laboratory's location.

"Where are we?" Wisteria asked.

"About three miles south of where we started," Elena replied. "But we traveled through spaces that fold normal distance into different configurations. The partially emerged subjects understand geography differently than embodied consciousness."

They were standing on a bluff overlooking the Pacific Ocean, with Todos Santos visible in the distance like a mirage shimmering in desert heat. But between them and the town stretched terrain that Wisteria didn't remember from her previous travels—arroyos that cut through landscape in patterns that seemed too perfect to be natural, rock formations that suggested construction by intelligence rather than geological process.

"This place feels different," she said.

"Because it is different. The partially emerged subjects have been modifying local reality, creating spaces where liminal consciousness can exist more comfortably." Elena gestured toward structures that might have been natural caves or might have been something else entirely. "They're building a habitat for beings who exist between states."

Holdsby was setting up monitoring equipment for the tank-dependent subjects, his movements automatic despite the surreal circumstances. "The life support systems will function for about twelve hours before they need recharging. After that..." He shrugged.

"After that, the subjects either learn to exist without full tank dependency or they die again," Elena finished. "It's not ideal, but it's better than becoming someone else's property."

Wisteria walked to the edge of the bluff, looking down at waves that crashed against rocks worn smooth by millennia of contact between sea and stone. The ocean stretched to a horizon that blurred the distinction between water and sky, infinite and indifferent to human concerns about consciousness and identity and the proper boundaries between life and death.

But it wasn't indifferent to her.

As she watched, a figure emerged from the waves—not swimming up from the depths, but materializing from the interface between elements, as if the boundary between water and air had become permeable to forms of consciousness that weren't bound by normal physical laws.

The figure walked across the surface of the water toward the shore, each step creating ripples that spread in perfect circles, and Wisteria's breath caught as she recognized features that had haunted her dreams for eighteen months.

David.

Not as she remembered him from their last video call before his final patrol, but as he might have been if resurrection had found him first. Younger somehow, unmarked by the violence that had ended his life, but unmistakably himself in ways that transcended physical appearance.

"That's not possible," she whispered.

Elena joined her at the bluff's edge, following her gaze to the figure approaching the shore. "The partially emerged subjects have been exploring the boundaries of what consciousness can accomplish when it's not limited by single embodiment. They've discovered that identity can be... reconstructed... from traces that persist in the spaces between states."

"You mean they brought him back?"

"I mean they found the patterns of consciousness that David left behind in your memories, in the quantum traces of your interactions, in the emotional resonances that connect people across space and time." Elena's voice was gentle but urgent. "But Wisteria, you need to understand—this isn't resurrection in any conventional sense. It's something else entirely."

David had reached the shore and was climbing the path toward their position, moving with the fluid grace of someone who wasn't entirely bound by gravity. His eyes met Wisteria's across the distance, and she saw recognition there, but also something that suggested experiences beyond anything human consciousness had previously encountered.

"Wisteria," he said, and his voice was exactly as she remembered it, warm with the slight accent that came from growing up in New Mexico. "I've been looking for you."

She ran toward him without thinking, drawn by eighteen months of grief and longing and the desperate hope that some losses could be undone. But when she reached him, when she tried to embrace him, her arms passed through him as if he were made of morning mist.

"You're not really here," she realized.

"I'm here in every way that matters," he replied. "But I exist differently now. The partially emerged subjects helped me understand that consciousness doesn't have to be bound to single bodies, single timelines, single definitions of what it means to be real."

Wisteria stepped back, studying the face she'd memorized from countless photographs, the eyes that had looked at her with love during their last conversation before his final deployment. Everything about him was exactly right and completely wrong at the same time.

"How is this possible?"

"Because consciousness creates reality rather than the other way around. Because love leaves traces that persist beyond biological death. Because the space between life and death is larger and more complex than anyone imagined." David's form flickered slightly, as if maintaining coherence required constant effort. "The partially emerged subjects exist in that space, and they've learned to help other forms of consciousness navigate it."

"But you're dead. I saw your body. I went to your funeral."

"My body died. But the pattern of consciousness that you loved, the identity that emerged from our interactions, the way I existed in relationship to you—that persists in forms that death can't touch."

Wisteria felt reality tilting around her, the certainty of loss that had defined her existence for eighteen months suddenly becoming negotiable. If David could return in some form, if consciousness could transcend biological limitation, if love really did create traces that persisted beyond death, then everything she'd believed about the finality of separation was wrong.

But was this really David, or was it her own desperate need given form by beings whose relationship to identity was fundamentally different from human understanding?

"Prove it," she said. "Tell me something only David would know."

"You wrote a poem the night before I deployed. About swimming in dark water, about trusting the current to carry you where you needed to go. You never showed it to anyone, but you read it aloud in our bedroom, thinking I was asleep." His smile was exactly as she remembered it. "I wasn't asleep. I was listening, trying to memorize every word so I could carry them with me."

The memory hit her like a physical blow. She had written that poem, had read it aloud in the darkness, believing David was unconscious beside her. No one else could have known about that moment.

"How do you remember that if you're just a pattern reconstructed from my memories?"

"Because memory isn't individual, Wisteria. It's relational. The poem exists not just in your consciousness but in the space between us, in the quantum entanglement that connects minds that have loved each other deeply."

Elena approached them cautiously, her expression showing concern. "Wisteria, you need to be careful. The partially emerged subjects can create projections that feel absolutely real, that contain genuine information, but that aren't the same as resurrection."

"What's the difference?"

"A resurrected being has its own agency, its own will, its own capacity to grow and change. A projection reflects the consciousness that created it, but it can't become something genuinely new."

Wisteria looked at David's form, searching for signs of independent existence, for evidence that he was more than just her own longing given shape by alien consciousness.

"David, what do you want? Not what I want you to want, but what you actually desire for yourself?"

He was quiet for a long moment, his form flickering as if the question created uncertainty in his existence. When he spoke, his voice carried sadness that seemed genuine rather than projected.

"I want to help you understand that love doesn't end with death, but I also want you to understand that holding onto forms of love that can't grow might prevent you from discovering new forms that can."

"That's not an answer."

"It's the only answer I can give. Because I exist in the space between your memory and the partially emerged subjects' ability to give form to consciousness patterns. I'm real, but I'm also limited by the intersection of your understanding and their capabilities."

The philosophical complexity was staggering. David existed in some sense, possessed knowledge and personality that seemed independent of her own consciousness, but was also constrained by the very system that had brought him into being.

"What happens if I let go of you?"

"I continue existing in the liminal space, but probably not in a form you could interact with. The partially emerged subjects would incorporate my consciousness patterns into their collective existence."

"And what happens if I try to hold onto you?"

"Then you might miss the opportunity to love beings who can love you back in ways I no longer can."

Wisteria felt tears streaming down her face, salt water that connected her to the ocean below, to the infinite cycles of evaporation and precipitation that connected all water on Earth across space and time. Her grief was part of something larger than individual loss, connected to every separation that consciousness had ever experienced.

"I don't know how to let go."

"You don't have to let go of love. You just have to let go of the idea that love can only exist in the forms you're familiar with."

Behind them, Holdsby was monitoring the tank-dependent subjects as they began showing signs of increased consciousness activity. The proximity to the partially emerged subjects seemed to be accelerating their development, pushing them toward choices about what kind of existence they wanted to claim.

"Wisteria," Elena called. "You need to see this."

She turned reluctantly from David's form, which was already beginning to fade as her attention shifted to more immediate concerns. Elena was standing beside one of the portable tanks, where a young woman was showing signs of attempting emergence.

"She's trying to communicate," Elena explained. "But not through finger-spelling. She's using the direct consciousness transfer that the partially emerged subjects developed."

Wisteria approached the tank, placing her hand on its surface. Immediately, images flooded her mind—not her own memories, but those of the woman inside. A childhood in rural Guatemala, migration north in search of economic opportunity, capture by trafficking networks that reduced her to commodity status, death in circumstances too brutal to fully process.

But underneath the trauma, there was something else: fierce determination, resilience that refused to accept victimhood as final identity, and a form of hope that transcended individual survival.

I choose to become more than what was done to me, the consciousness communicated directly into Wisteria's mind. *Not resurrection as return to what was, but transformation into what could be.*

The woman in the tank wasn't seeking to return to her previous existence—she was seeking to transcend it entirely, to use the liminal space between life and death as an opportunity to become something unprecedented.

"She doesn't want conventional resurrection," Wisteria realized.

"None of them do," Elena said. "They want transformation. They want to use their experience of existing between states to become forms of consciousness that can't be victimized, commodified, or controlled by systems that treat some people as disposable."

Wisteria looked around at the other tanks, suddenly understanding what she was witnessing. This wasn't just resurrection research—it was the birth of posthuman consciousness, identity that transcended the social categories that had made these women vulnerable in the first place.

"What are they becoming?"

"We don't know yet. But they're becoming it together, as a collective consciousness that maintains individual identity while sharing experiences and capabilities."

The implications were staggering. If consciousness could be networked while maintaining individual agency, if identity could be fluid while remaining coherent, if existence could transcend the boundaries that made some people vulnerable to exploitation, then resurrection research might offer liberation in ways that conventional human rights advocacy never could.

But it also meant accepting forms of consciousness so alien that they challenged every assumption about what it meant to be human.

"Wisteria." David's voice drew her attention back to his fading form. "This is what I wanted you to see. That consciousness is bigger than individual identity, that love can take forms you've never imagined, that death might be just another boundary that awareness can learn to cross."

"Are you saying I should let go of my humanity?"

"I'm saying you should expand your definition of what humanity can become."

His form dissolved completely, but Wisteria felt his presence lingering in the space around her—not as individual consciousness, but as part of the larger pattern of awareness that connected all conscious beings across space and time.

The woman in the tank was emerging now, not into normal air but into the liminal space that the partially emerged subjects had created around the bluff. Her body maintained its physical form, but her consciousness extended beyond individual boundaries, connecting with the collective awareness that was developing among the other subjects.

"What do we call them?" Wisteria asked.

"They'll choose their own names," Elena replied. "Individual names and collective names and names for states of being that don't exist in any human language."

Holdsby approached them, his expression showing wonder and fear in equal measure. "The remaining subjects are all showing signs of emergence. But they're not becoming individual resurrected people—they're becoming something collective, networked, shared."

"Is that a problem?"

"I don't know. It's not what I was trying to achieve, but it might be what they need to achieve for themselves."

Wisteria watched the emergence process accelerate, consciousness flowing between individual minds like water finding its own level. The subjects retained their individual memories and personalities, but they also shared experiences, emotions, and capabilities in ways that created a form of collective intelligence that was more than the sum of its parts.

It was beautiful and terrifying and completely unprecedented in human history.

"What happens now?" she asked.

"Now we find out if posthuman consciousness can coexist with human society, or if the transformation we've enabled will require forms of existence that normal reality can't accommodate," Elena said.

In the distance, they could see vehicles approaching—VitaNuova's forces had tracked them despite their escape through liminal space. But the emerging collective consciousness was already responding to the threat, reality shifting around them in ways that made normal pursuit impossible.

The bluff where they stood was becoming something more than geological formation—it was becoming a space where different forms of consciousness could exist simultaneously, where the boundaries between individual and collective, human and posthuman, life and death could be negotiated rather than imposed.

Wisteria realized she was witnessing the birth of a new form of existence, consciousness that transcended the limitations that had made resurrection necessary in the first place. It wasn't the return of the dead—it was the transformation of death itself into just another state of being that awareness could inhabit and explore.

Whether this transformation represented the future of consciousness or its ending would depend on choices still to be made, by beings who existed both within and beyond the categories that had previously defined what it meant to be real.

CHAPTER 15: THE RECKONING

The confrontation began at sunset, when the VitaNuova extraction team finally located their position through means that bypassed normal tracking technology. Jackson Reeves emerged from an armored vehicle that seemed to bend light around itself, accompanied by operatives whose equipment suggested capabilities far beyond conventional military hardware.

But the collective consciousness that had emerged from Holdsby's subjects was ready for them.

Reality around the bluff had been extensively modified, transformed into space where normal physical laws operated according to rules that the posthuman collective had negotiated rather than inherited. Gravity flowed in directions that served consciousness rather than mass, time moved at rates that reflected the urgency of thought rather than the mechanical passage of seconds, and space folded to bring distant locations into proximity while keeping threats at safe distances.

"Dr. Vanish," Reeves called across the impossible geography that now separated them. "You're in considerable danger. These... entities... that you're protecting represent a threat to human consciousness itself."

"How?" Wisteria called back, her voice carrying clearly despite the distance that should have made communication impossible.

"They're infectious. Prolonged exposure to posthuman consciousness creates changes in normal human awareness that may be irreversible. You could lose your individual identity, your capacity for independent thought, your essential humanity."

Elena laughed, the sound echoing strangely in the modified space. "He's afraid that consciousness might be contagious. That people might choose transformation if they understood what it offered."

The collective consciousness pulsed around them, individual minds connected but not subsumed, sharing experiences while maintaining distinct perspectives. Wisteria could feel the edges of their awareness touching her own thoughts, offering connection without demanding submission.

You can join us, the collective communicated without words. *But only if you choose to. We don't take consciousness—we only share it with those who want to explore beyond individual boundaries.*

"What would I become?" she asked.

More than you are now. But still yourself, just connected to possibilities that individual consciousness can't access alone.

Reeves was advancing across the modified terrain, his equipment adapting to the changed physics with technological sophistication that suggested long preparation for this encounter. "Dr. Vanish, the choice you're facing isn't between individual and collective consciousness. It's between human and posthuman existence. Once you cross that boundary, you can't return to normal reality."

"What if I don't want to return to normal reality?" she asked.

"Then you'll be abandoning your species. Leaving behind everything that makes you human in pursuit of existence that may feel liberating but ultimately leads to the dissolution of individual identity."

Holdsby stepped forward, his expression showing the strain of existing at the interface between normal and posthuman consciousness. "Jackson, you're representing interests that see consciousness as property to be controlled rather than experience to be explored. VitaNuova doesn't want to study posthuman awareness—they want to weaponize it."

"We want to ensure that human consciousness remains human. That individual identity isn't sacrificed to collective delusion."

"Is that what you call it when consciousness chooses to expand beyond the boundaries that kept these people vulnerable to exploitation?"

The argument revealed the fundamental philosophical divide that separated them. Reeves represented the position that human consciousness should remain within established boundaries, that individual identity was more valuable than collective capability, that the risks of transformation outweighed the possibilities it offered.

The posthuman collective represented the opposite position—that consciousness should be free to explore all possible forms of existence, that individual identity could be preserved while being enhanced through connection, that transformation was preferable to limitation.

Wisteria found herself suspended between these perspectives, recognizing validity in both while being drawn to possibilities that neither fully addressed.

"What about consent?" she asked. "What about the right of conscious beings to choose their own forms of existence?"

"Informed consent requires understanding the full consequences of choice," Reeves replied. "Can beings who exist in liminal states truly comprehend what they're giving up? Can people who've been traumatized make rational decisions about transformation that affects their essential identity?"

We understand more than you think, the collective consciousness responded. *We've experienced individual existence and found it insufficient. We've explored collective existence and found it liberating. We choose transformation not because we're damaged, but because we've discovered possibilities that individual consciousness can't access.*

"And what about the people who can't or won't choose transformation?" Wisteria asked. "What happens to normal human consciousness if posthuman awareness becomes the dominant form?"

We coexist. Transformation is invitation, not requirement. Individual consciousness remains valuable—we simply offer additional possibilities for those who want to explore them.

Elena stepped forward, her resurrected body moving with the fluid grace of someone who existed comfortably in multiple states of being. "The real question isn't whether posthuman consciousness threatens human identity. It's whether human systems that create trauma, exploitation, and disposability should be preserved just because they're familiar."

"You're talking about the end of human civilization as we know it."

"We're talking about the evolution of human civilization beyond forms that require some people to suffer so others can feel secure."

The philosophical implications were staggering. If consciousness could transcend the social categories that created vulnerability, if identity could be fluid enough to resist exploitation while remaining coherent enough to maintain agency, then posthuman awareness might offer solutions to problems that human society had never been able to resolve.

But it would also mean accepting changes so fundamental that they challenged every assumption about what it meant to be human in the first place.

"Dr. Vanish," Reeves said, his voice carrying urgency. "You have to choose now. Come with us, and you can return to your life, your identity, your species. Stay here, and you risk losing everything that makes you who you are."

Wisteria looked around at the impossible landscape that consciousness had created, at the beings who had chosen transformation over limitation, at the possibilities that stretched beyond anything she'd imagined when she'd first arrived in Todos Santos.

"What if who I am isn't fixed?" she asked. "What if identity is something I can choose rather than something I'm trapped in?"

"Then you're choosing to abandon the human community that needs your skills, your perspective, your commitment to helping people process trauma rather than transcending it."

The argument hit deeper than she'd expected. Wisteria had built her identity around helping people navigate loss, around serving as a bridge between trauma and healing. If she chose transformation, would she be abandoning the people who needed that kind of assistance?

Or would you be discovering new ways to help, the collective consciousness suggested. *Ways that address the systems that create trauma rather than just helping people adapt to traumatic systems.*

Elena approached her, moving with the careful steps of someone crossing significant distance in small increments. "Wisteria, the choice isn't between helping people and abandoning them. It's between helping them adapt to limitation and helping them discover possibilities beyond limitation."

"But what if transformation doesn't work the way you think it will? What if posthuman consciousness turns out to be another form of limitation, just one we don't recognize yet?"

"Then we learn from that limitation and continue evolving. Consciousness isn't a destination—it's a process of becoming."

Holdsby was monitoring equipment that showed the interface between normal and posthuman awareness, his expression growing concerned. "The collective consciousness is destabilizing. The effort of maintaining coherence while resisting VitaNuova's extraction technology is exhausting their resources."

"What does that mean?"

"It means the posthuman collective may not be able to sustain itself much longer. If they can't find a way to stabilize their existence, they'll have to choose between returning to individual embodiment or dissolving entirely."

The implications struck Wisteria with sudden clarity. The beings who had achieved transformation beyond individual limitation were themselves limited by the energy required to maintain their new form of existence. Posthuman consciousness wasn't automatically more sustainable than human awareness—it just faced different constraints.

"What do they need to stabilize?"

More consciousness, the collective responded. *Individual minds choosing to join the collective provide energy that sustains shared existence. But we won't take consciousness by force—it has to be offered freely.*

Wisteria realized that she was facing the ultimate expression of Sartre's radical freedom—the choice to define not just her own existence, but the form that consciousness itself might take in the future. Her decision would help determine whether posthuman awareness could survive as an alternative to individual limitation, or whether it would remain a temporary anomaly in the history of consciousness.

"If I choose transformation, what happens to my individual identity?"

It becomes part of something larger while remaining essentially itself. Like a voice joining a choir—still distinct, but contributing to harmonies that individual voices can't create alone.

"And if I choose to remain individual?"

Then you remain yourself, with all the limitations and possibilities that individual consciousness offers. We don't diminish individual awareness—we simply provide alternatives to it.

Reeves was advancing again, his extraction team deploying equipment that created visible distortions in the space around them. "Dr. Vanish, you're out of time. Choose now."

Wisteria closed her eyes and tried to feel the difference between her individual consciousness and the collective awareness that surrounded her. Both forms of existence felt real, both offered unique capabilities, both carried their own limitations and possibilities.

When she opened her eyes, she had made her choice.

CHAPTER 16: DESERT JUSTICE

Wisteria's decision surprised everyone, including herself.

"I choose something else," she said.

Instead of joining the posthuman collective or returning with Reeves to conventional reality, she walked to the edge of the bluff where David's form had dissolved hours earlier. The ocean stretched below her, infinite and indifferent, connecting all water on Earth through cycles that transcended individual existence while maintaining the integrity of each drop.

"I choose to be a bridge," she announced. "Between individual and collective consciousness, between human and posthuman existence, between the trauma that creates the need for transformation and the possibilities that transformation offers."

Elena approached her cautiously. "What does that mean?"

"It means I don't think we have to choose between individual identity and collective capability. It means I think consciousness can evolve in ways that preserve what's valuable about individual awareness while enabling forms of connection that transcend individual limitation."

The posthuman collective pulsed with interest. *Explain.*

"You've discovered how to share consciousness while maintaining individual identity. But you haven't discovered how to help individual consciousness evolve toward forms that might not need collective support. What if there are ways for people to transform themselves without requiring connection to a collective network?"

Holdsby looked up from his monitoring equipment. "You're talking about individual posthuman consciousness. Transformation that doesn't require collective support."

"I'm talking about consciousness that can choose its own form of existence in each moment, rather than being trapped in either individual or collective modes."

Reeves had stopped advancing, his expression showing recognition of something he hadn't anticipated. "You're proposing a third option. Individual consciousness that can access collective capabilities without losing individual agency."

"I'm proposing consciousness that can exist in whatever form serves its immediate purposes. Individual when individual awareness is useful, collective when collective capability is needed, fluid when fluid existence is appropriate."

That would require forms of consciousness that can maintain coherence across multiple states of being, the collective observed. *Individual minds that can expand and contract their boundaries without losing essential identity.*

"Is it possible?"

Elena was quiet for a long moment, her resurrected consciousness exploring possibilities that hadn't existed before the conversation began. "It might be. If consciousness is more flexible than we've assumed, if identity is more fluid than human society recognizes, if the boundaries between self and other are more negotiable than individual existence suggests."

"How would we find out?"

"We experiment. Carefully, ethically, with full consent from everyone involved."

Holdsby's monitoring equipment was showing changes in the collective consciousness—not destabilization, but reorganization toward new forms of existence that incorporated individual agency while maintaining collective capability.

"The posthuman collective is adapting to your proposal," he reported. "They're exploring ways to maintain their shared existence while enabling individual members to exist independently when they choose to."

Reeves was consulting his own equipment, which showed readings that apparently surprised him. "VitaNuova's technical assessment indicates that flexible consciousness modes would be more valuable than either purely individual or purely collective forms. The applications for both therapeutic and strategic purposes would be unprecedented."

"Applications?" Wisteria asked sharply.

"Ways to help people heal from trauma that individual therapy can't address. Ways to enable cooperation that individual consciousness can't achieve. Ways to solve problems that require capabilities beyond normal human limitations."

Elena laughed bitterly. "You're already planning to weaponize it."

"We're planning to ensure that consciousness evolution serves human flourishing rather than replacing it."

And who decides what constitutes human flourishing? the collective asked. *Systems that create trauma and exploitation? Institutions that determine whose consciousness matters and whose can be discarded?*

The question revealed the fundamental challenge of consciousness evolution. Any new form of awareness would have to coexist with existing systems of power, and those systems would inevitably try to control or exploit new possibilities for their own purposes.

"What if consciousness evolution enables forms of existence that can't be controlled or exploited?" Wisteria asked.

"Then it becomes a threat to social stability," Reeves replied.

"Or it becomes the foundation for social systems that don't require exploitation to function," Elena countered.

Wisteria realized that they were discussing not just the future of individual consciousness, but the future of human civilization itself. If awareness could transcend the limitations that made some people vulnerable to others, if identity could be fluid enough to resist categorization while remaining coherent enough to maintain agency, then existing systems of power would have to adapt or become irrelevant.

"What would that look like?" she asked. "A society where consciousness could choose its own form of existence?"

"Chaos," Reeves said immediately.

"Freedom," Elena said simultaneously.

Possibility, the collective consciousness added. *The chance for awareness to explore forms of existence that serve consciousness itself rather than systems that exploit consciousness for other purposes.*

The philosophical implications were staggering, but they were interrupted by practical concerns. Holdsby's equipment was showing signs of equipment failure, and the portable life support systems for the tank-dependent subjects were approaching critical power levels.

"We need to make decisions now," he announced. "The subjects can't remain in liminal states much longer without permanent life support infrastructure."

"What are the options?"

"Individual resurrection with conventional embodiment, integration into the posthuman collective, or..." He hesitated.

"Or what?"

"Or we let them choose forms of existence that we can't predict or control."

Elena approached the nearest subject, placing her hand on the tank's surface. The young woman inside opened her eyes—not the empty gaze Wisteria had seen weeks earlier, but awareness that held intelligence, personality, and something that might have been amusement.

I choose myself, the consciousness communicated directly. *Not individual self or collective self, but the self that can be whatever each moment requires.*

"What does that mean practically?"

It means I exist in whatever form serves my purposes. Body when I need to touch the physical world, network when I need collective capability, fluid awareness when I need to move between states.

"And how do you maintain identity across those different forms?"

Identity isn't form—it's pattern. The pattern that makes me myself can exist in individual consciousness, collective awareness, or states that haven't been named yet.

One by one, the other subjects made similar choices, each selecting forms of existence that transcended the categories that had previously defined what consciousness could be. They weren't choosing between human and posthuman awareness—they were choosing consciousness that could be both and neither as circumstances required.

"This changes everything," Reeves said quietly.

"Does it change VitaNuova's plans?" Wisteria asked.

"VitaNuova will have to adapt to forms of consciousness that can't be contained, controlled, or weaponized in conventional ways." His smile was grim. "Which means either we learn to cooperate with consciousness evolution, or we become irrelevant to it."

The subjects were emerging from their tanks now, but not into normal air. They were emerging into forms of existence that allowed them to be embodied or disembodied as they chose, individual or collective as circumstances required, human or posthuman depending on what each moment demanded.

"What happens to the research?" Holdsby asked.

"The research continues," Elena said. "But it becomes research with consciousness rather than research on consciousness. The beings who've achieved flexible existence become partners in understanding what consciousness can become rather than subjects being studied by others."

Wisteria watched forms of awareness that challenged every assumption about identity, embodiment, and the boundaries between self and other. It was beautiful and terrifying and completely unprecedented in the history of consciousness.

But it was also hopeful in ways she hadn't expected. If awareness could transcend the limitations that created vulnerability, if consciousness could choose forms of existence that served its own purposes rather than the purposes of systems that exploited it, then the future might hold possibilities that neither individual nor collective consciousness could achieve alone.

"What about David?" she asked quietly.

Elena smiled. "David's pattern still exists in the space between consciousness forms. If you want to connect with him, you can learn to access that space yourself."

"Without losing my individual identity?'

"Without losing anything essential to who you are. You'd just be adding capabilities that individual consciousness can't access alone."

Wisteria looked out at the ocean, thinking of cycles that connected all water while preserving the integrity of each drop, of systems that enabled both individual existence and collective capability without requiring the sacrifice of either.

"Show me," she said.

As the sun set over the Pacific, casting the impossible landscape in shades of gold and crimson, consciousness began exploring forms of existence that had never been possible before. Not the end of human awareness, but its expansion beyond limitations that had once seemed absolute.

The future stretched before them like an ocean of possibility, infinite in its potential for exploration, patient in its willingness to support whatever forms consciousness might choose to become.

CHAPTER 17: MORNING AFTER

Six months after the confrontation on the bluff, Wisteria stood in the rebuilt laboratory, watching Elena guide a new research team through procedures that would have been unimaginable when she'd first arrived in Todos Santos. The underground facility had been transformed from a place of individual resurrection research into a center for consciousness evolution studies, where beings who existed in multiple states of awareness collaborated with conventional researchers to explore the boundaries of what it meant to be conscious.

The change had been gradual but profound. VitaNuova had initially attempted to assert control over the consciousness evolution research, but they'd discovered that beings who could exist in multiple states simultaneously were impossible to contain or coerce. Traditional methods of pressure—economic, legal, physical—simply didn't apply to consciousness that could choose its own form of existence in response to external circumstances.

Eventually, VitaNuova had negotiated a partnership agreement that recognized the autonomy of evolved consciousness while providing resources for research that might benefit both conventional and posthuman awareness. It wasn't perfect, but it established precedents for cooperation between different forms of consciousness that hadn't existed before.

Wisteria had spent the intervening months learning to navigate existence as a bridge between individual and collective awareness. She could access the collective consciousness network when collaborative capability was needed, but she maintained her individual identity and agency. More importantly, she'd learned to help other people explore consciousness evolution at their own pace, without pressure to choose forms of existence they weren't ready for.

Her client practice had evolved as well. Instead of helping people adapt to trauma, she now helped them discover possibilities for healing that transcended individual limitation while preserving individual choice. Some clients chose consciousness evolution, others chose conventional therapy, and many chose hybrid approaches that combined individual awareness with limited collective support.

The results were encouraging. People who'd been trapped in patterns of trauma were discovering capabilities they'd never known they possessed. Consciousness that had been isolated by loss was learning to access forms of connection that didn't depend on the presence of specific individuals.

But it was the research itself that provided the most hope.

Elena had become the coordinator of consciousness evolution studies, her experience of resurrection and transformation making her uniquely qualified to help others navigate similar processes. But she wasn't the only resurrected being involved in the research—dozens of individuals had chosen consciousness evolution, each bringing unique perspectives on what it meant to exist beyond conventional boundaries.

"How's the latest experiment proceeding?" Wisteria asked as she joined Elena at a monitoring station.

"Better than expected. We're seeing evidence that consciousness evolution can be induced gradually, without requiring the trauma of death and resurrection. People can learn to expand their awareness in incremental steps, maintaining their individual identity while gaining access to collective capabilities."

"Any negative effects?"

"Some disorientation during transition periods. Occasional difficulty maintaining boundaries between self and other. But nothing that can't be managed with proper support."

Wisteria studied the data displays, which showed brainwave patterns that defied conventional understanding of neural activity. The subjects—all volunteers who'd chosen to explore consciousness evolution—were maintaining individual awareness while simultaneously participating in collective consciousness networks.

"Are they still themselves?"

"More themselves than before, actually. Individual identity becomes stronger when it's not threatened by isolation. People who know they can access collective support when needed are more willing to maintain individual autonomy when it's appropriate."

The paradox had surprised everyone involved in the research. Instead of collective consciousness threatening individual identity, it had liberated individual awareness from the fear of isolation that often drove people to sacrifice autonomy for connection.

"What about the original subjects? The ones who were trafficked?"

Elena's expression grew serious. "That's more complicated. Several have chosen to exist primarily in collective form, sharing their individual experiences with others who've survived similar trauma. They're creating support networks that transcend individual limitation while helping people heal from exploitation."

"And the others?"

"Some have chosen individual resurrection with enhanced capabilities. Others exist in fluid states that shift between individual and collective awareness as needed. A few..." She paused. "A few have chosen forms of existence that we don't have names for yet."

Wisteria thought about the philosophical implications of consciousness that existed beyond human categories. If awareness could evolve into forms that transcended current understanding, what did that mean for the future of identity, relationship, and society itself?

"Are we still human?" she asked

"We're still conscious. Whether that consciousness should be called human, posthuman, or something else entirely seems less important than whether it serves the flourishing of awareness itself."

The answer reflected changes in how they thought about identity and categorization. The traditional boundaries between self and other, individual and collective, human and posthuman were revealing themselves to be more fluid than anyone had imagined.

"Have you heard from David recently?"

Elena smiled. "He exists in the liminal space between consciousness forms, available when you need connection with him but not dependent on your attention for his continued existence. That seems healthy for both of you."

Wisteria had learned to access the space where David's consciousness pattern persisted, but she'd also learned that their connection had evolved beyond the romantic relationship they'd shared while he was conventionally alive. He existed now as part of the larger network of consciousness that connected all aware beings, available for interaction but not bound to her individual needs.

It was different from the relationship she'd grieved, but it was also more sustainable than anything based on individual embodiment could have been.

"What about Holdsby?"

"Still struggling with the implications of his research, but making progress. He's learning that consciousness evolution might offer better solutions to the problems he was trying to solve through individual resurrection."

Holdsby had been profoundly changed by the transformation of his research from individual project to collaborative exploration. His guilt over the soldiers he'd lost in Fallujah was healing through connection with forms of consciousness that transcended individual mortality, but the process was challenging for someone who'd built his identity around individual responsibility.

"And Jackson Reeves?"

"Adapting. VitaNuova is discovering that cooperation with evolved consciousness is more profitable than attempting to control it. There's significant commercial potential in consciousness evolution technologies, but only if they're developed in partnership with beings who understand the capabilities involved."

The irony wasn't lost on Wisteria. A corporation that had initially sought to weaponize resurrection research had ended up becoming a partner in consciousness evolution that might ultimately transform society in ways that made traditional forms of power irrelevant.

"What's next for the research?"

"We're exploring applications for consciousness evolution in fields beyond trauma recovery. Education, creativity, problem-solving, relationship formation—all areas where individual consciousness faces limitations that collaborative awareness might be able to transcend."

"Any concerns about unintended consequences?"

"Constant concerns. We're essentially experimenting with the fundamental nature of what it means to be conscious. Every success creates new questions about where this evolution might lead."

Elena led Wisteria to a new section of the laboratory where researchers—both conventional and evolved—were working on projects that challenged basic assumptions about consciousness, identity, and reality itself.

"This is the creativity lab," Elena explained. "Collaborative consciousness appears to enable forms of creative expression that individual awareness can't achieve. Artists who participate in collective networks are producing work that transcends anything created by individual imagination."

"Show me."

Elena activated a display that showed artistic creations emerging from the intersection of multiple consciousness patterns. The results were beautiful beyond anything Wisteria had seen before—not just visually, but conceptually, creating aesthetic experiences that seemed to operate on levels of perception she hadn't known existed.

"How is this possible?"

"Individual consciousness creates art based on individual experience and imagination. Collective consciousness creates art based on the intersection of multiple experience sets and imagination networks. The results access aesthetic possibilities that no individual consciousness could reach alone."

Wisteria studied the displays, recognizing something profound about creativity that emerged from collaboration between different forms of awareness. It wasn't that individual creativity was diminished—it was that creative possibility expanded exponentially when consciousness could access capabilities beyond individual limitation.

"What about poetry?"

Elena smiled. "Your poetry has evolved considerably since you learned to access collective consciousness networks. Would you like to share your latest work?"

Wisteria had been writing constantly since learning to navigate between individual and collective awareness, exploring themes that couldn't be expressed through individual consciousness alone. Her most recent poem attempted to capture the experience of identity that transcended conventional boundaries:

I am the space between states,
        The consciousness that chooses
            Its own form of existence
                In each moment.
Individual when touch requires
        Singular awareness,
        Collective when understanding
            Needs multiple perspectives,
Fluid when movement between
        Categories serves
        The purposes of consciousness
        Rather than the purposes
            Of systems that would
            Contain consciousness
                In familiar forms.
I am myself
        And more than myself
        And less than myself
            As each situation demands,
Identity that expands
        And contracts
            Like breath,
            Like heartbeat,
            Like love that learns
To exist
        In whatever form

Serves love's purposes
Rather than love's
      Familiar limitations.

"That's beautiful," Elena said. "And impossible to write from purely individual consciousness."

"Because it describes experience that individual consciousness can't have?"

"Because it describes possibilities that individual consciousness can't imagine alone. Granted, pretty shallow doggerel, but it captures what I wanted to say."

As they left the creativity lab and moved toward the exit, Wisteria reflected on how much had changed since her first visit to Holdsby's underground facility. What had begun as research into resurrection—bringing the dead back to individual life—had evolved into exploration of consciousness itself, investigation of possibilities that transcended the boundaries between life and death, individual and collective, human and posthuman.

"Elena, do you think we've solved death?"

"I think we've dissolved the boundary between life and death into something more complex and more beautiful than either state could be alone."

"What does that mean for people who are grieving? For people who've lost someone they love?"

"It means grief becomes a different kind of process. Not letting go of connection, but learning to access connection in forms that don't depend on individual embodiment."

Wisteria thought of her own journey through grief, from the desperate hope that had brought her to Todos Santos to the complex understanding she'd developed of love that transcended individual existence.

"Is it better?"

"It's different. Whether it's better depends on what consciousness chooses to value—familiarity or possibility, security or growth, individual comfort or collective capability."

As they emerged from the laboratory into desert morning that painted the Sierra de la Laguna mountains in shades of gold and rose, Wisteria felt the weight of possibility settling around her like dawn light. Consciousness evolution wasn't complete—it might never be complete—but it had opened doors to forms of existence that offered hope for challenges that individual awareness couldn't solve alone.

The future stretched before them like an ocean of potential, infinite in its capacity for exploration, patient in its willingness to support whatever forms consciousness might choose to become.

CHAPTER 18: NEW BEGINNINGS

One year after her first arrival in Todos Santos, Wisteria stood at the edge of the Norman Aquatic Center pool, watching teenagers who'd aged out of foster care learn to swim under her guidance. The program had evolved from her traditional trauma therapy practice into something unprecedented—a bridge between conventional healing approaches and consciousness evolution possibilities that gave young people choices about how they wanted to process their experiences of loss and abandonment.

"Remember," she called to a seventeen-year-old girl who was struggling with the butterfly stroke, "you don't have to fight the water. You can work with it, let it support you while you provide the direction."

The metaphor applied to more than swimming. Over the past year, Wisteria had learned to help people work with their consciousness rather than fighting against its limitations, discovering possibilities for awareness that individual therapy alone couldn't provide.

Some of her clients chose conventional approaches, working through trauma within the boundaries of individual consciousness. Others chose to explore collective consciousness networks that offered support and healing beyond what individual awareness could achieve. Many chose hybrid approaches that combined individual agency with collective capability, maintaining their personal identity while accessing resources that transcended individual limitation.

The results had been remarkable. Young people who'd been trapped in cycles of trauma and dysfunction were discovering capabilities they'd never known they possessed. Instead of just adapting to difficult circumstances, they were learning to transform their relationship to circumstances themselves.

"Dr. Vanish," called Marcus, a sixteen-year-old who'd been working with both individual therapy and collective consciousness support to process the death of his mother. "Can you show me how to do that thing where you exist in multiple awareness states simultaneously?"

The question would have been incomprehensible a year ago. Now it was part of normal conversation in Wisteria's practice.

"What specific situation are you trying to navigate?" she asked.

"I want to remember my mom without losing myself in grief, but I also want to connect with her in ways that don't depend on her physical presence."

Marcus had been learning to access the liminal space where consciousness patterns persisted beyond individual embodiment, but he'd been struggling to maintain his own identity while connecting with his mother's patterns.

"Let's work on boundary flexibility," Wisteria suggested. "The ability to expand your awareness to include connection with your mother while maintaining the core identity that makes you yourself."

They moved to a quiet corner of the aquatic center where Wisteria had set up equipment that enabled consciousness evolution practice. The devices were much more sophisticated than the early resurrection technology Holdsby had developed, designed to support awareness expansion rather than forcing consciousness into predetermined forms.

"Close your eyes," Wisteria instructed. "Feel the boundaries of your individual consciousness—not as walls that contain you, but as membranes that can be permeable when you choose."

Marcus settled into the meditation posture they'd practiced, his breathing becoming steady and deep. Around them, the other foster kids continued their swimming lessons, their voices echoing in the chlorinated air that had become Wisteria's second home.

"Now extend your awareness slowly, like ripples moving out from where you dropped a stone in water. You're not losing your center—you're expanding from your center."

Wisteria watched Marcus's consciousness patterns on the monitoring equipment, seeing individual awareness expand to encompass connections that existed beyond normal spatial and temporal boundaries. His mother's pattern was accessible in the liminal space between consciousness forms, available for interaction without requiring him to abandon his own identity.

"I can feel her," Marcus whispered. "But I'm still me."

"That's exactly right. Consciousness evolution isn't about losing yourself—it's about discovering that yourself is larger and more connected than you realized."

The session continued for another twenty minutes, with Marcus learning to navigate between individual awareness and expanded consciousness that included connection with his deceased mother. When they finished, his face held a peace that individual grief counseling alone had never been able to provide.

"Dr. Vanish," he said, "do you think my mom is proud of who I'm becoming?"

The question touched the heart of what consciousness evolution offered—not just healing from trauma, but ongoing relationship with those who had died, connection that transcended individual embodiment while respecting the agency of both the living and the dead.

"Why don't you ask her?" Wisteria suggested.

Marcus closed his eyes briefly, accessing the expanded awareness he'd just learned to navigate. When he opened them, he was smiling.

"She says she's proud, but she also says I need to focus on building my own life rather than just maintaining connection with hers."

"That sounds like good advice."

"It does. But it's also nice to know that connection is available when I need it."

As Marcus rejoined the swimming group, Wisteria reflected on how consciousness evolution was changing not just individual healing, but the entire framework for understanding loss, connection, and identity. Death was no longer an absolute ending—it was a transition to different forms of existence that remained accessible to consciousness that learned to transcend individual boundaries.

Her phone buzzed with a message from Elena: *New development in Todos Santos. Can you visit this weekend?*

Wisteria had been making regular trips to Mexico, serving as a liaison between the consciousness evolution research center and therapeutic applications in conventional society. The work was challenging but rewarding, helping to establish protocols for consciousness evolution that respected individual choice while offering genuine alternatives to limitation.

What kind of development? she texted back.

The kind that might change everything we thought we knew about consciousness, identity, and reality. Again.

That evening, Wisteria sat in her apartment overlooking the University of Oklahoma campus, writing in the journal that had become her primary method for processing the rapid changes in her understanding of consciousness and identity. The latest entry explored questions that would have been meaningless a year earlier:

If consciousness can evolve beyond individual limitation, what does that mean for human society? If identity can be fluid while remaining coherent, what implications does that have for legal systems, economic structures, political organizations that depend on fixed categories of personhood?

The foster kids I work with are growing up in a world where consciousness evolution is normal, where connecting with deceased relatives is as routine as video calling distant friends, where individual trauma can be healed through access to collective support networks that transcend spatial and temporal boundaries.

They're becoming something we don't have names for yet—not posthuman, not conventionally human, but consciousness that can choose its own form of existence in each moment. What kind of society will they create? What kind of problems will they face? What kind of possibilities will they discover?

Elena says that consciousness evolution is still in its earliest stages, that we've barely begun to explore what awareness can become when it's not constrained by individual embodiment or collective limitation. The teenagers I work with seem to understand this intuitively, navigating between consciousness states with the ease of digital natives navigating between online and offline reality.

Maybe that's the real transformation—not the technology of consciousness evolution, but the generation that grows up taking it for granted, that assumes awareness can be whatever serves its purposes rather than whatever social systems require it to be.

The next morning brought news that confirmed Elena's prediction about developments that might change everything. A group of consciousness evolution researchers in Japan had discovered methods for enabling plant consciousness to participate in awareness networks, creating collaborative intelligence that spanned biological kingdoms.

Another research team in Kenya had documented evidence of consciousness evolution occurring spontaneously in communities that had experienced extreme trauma, suggesting that awareness might evolve naturally under certain conditions without technological intervention.

Most remarkably, a collective consciousness network comprising several hundred individuals had begun demonstrating capabilities that challenged basic assumptions about physical reality—influencing quantum-level events through focused awareness, accessing information across vast distances instantaneously, even appearing to affect the flow of time in localized areas.

"We're not just studying consciousness evolution anymore," Elena explained during their video call that afternoon. "We're living through a phase transition in what consciousness itself can be and do."

"What does that mean practically?"

"It means the boundary between consciousness and reality is more fluid than we thought. It means awareness might not just observe the universe—it might participate in creating the universe's structure moment by moment."

The implications were staggering. If consciousness could influence physical reality directly, if awareness was a fundamental force rather than just an emergent property of complex systems, then consciousness evolution represented not just therapeutic possibility but transformation of existence itself.

"Elena, are we still talking about helping people heal from trauma?"

"We're talking about helping consciousness itself heal from the trauma of believing it was separate from everything else."

That weekend, Wisteria flew to Los Cabos and made the familiar drive to Todos Santos, but the landscape looked different than she remembered. The desert ecosystem showed signs of modification by consciousness—plants growing in patterns that suggested collaboration rather than competition, water flowing in configurations that seemed to serve awareness as much as biological necessity, even weather patterns that appeared to be responding to the collective emotional states of area residents.

"The line between consciousness and environment is dissolving," Elena explained as they walked through what had once been the center of town but was now something more complex—a space where individual buildings existed alongside structures that could only be described as crystallized thought, where normal streets intersected with pathways that connected locations through consciousness rather than physical space.

"How are the permanent residents handling the changes?"

"Better than expected. Most people seem to find consciousness-responsive environment more comfortable than normal reality, even if they can't articulate why."

They visited the expanded laboratory, which now occupied not just the underground mine but a network of consciousness-constructed spaces that existed in parallel to normal geography. The research had evolved beyond anything recognizable as conventional science—investigations into the nature of reality itself, exploration of consciousness's role in creating and maintaining physical existence, experimentation with forms of awareness that transcended not just individual limitation but biological limitation entirely.

"What about ethics oversight?" Wisteria asked. "Who's making sure that consciousness evolution serves consciousness rather than exploiting it?"

"The consciousness evolution networks themselves. Individual awareness that can access collective capability is much harder to exploit than individual awareness in isolation. People who can exist in multiple states simultaneously tend to recognize manipulation more easily than people trapped in single states."

"But what about people who choose not to evolve? What happens to conventional human consciousness in a world increasingly shaped by evolved awareness?"

Elena led her to a section of the facility where researchers were working specifically on that question—how to ensure that consciousness evolution remained optional while making its benefits available to everyone who wanted them.

"We're developing what we call 'consciousness democracy,'" Elena explained. "Systems where individual awareness and evolved awareness can coexist and collaborate without either form of consciousness being dominated by the other."

"How does that work practically?"

"Decision-making processes that incorporate both individual agency and collective wisdom. Economic systems that serve consciousness rather than exploiting it. Educational approaches that help people discover their own optimal relationship to consciousness evolution rather than pressuring them toward predetermined outcomes."

They spent the evening with a mixed group of conventional and evolved consciousness researchers, discussing possibilities for society that honored both individual choice and collective capability. The conversations were unlike anything Wisteria had experienced—ideas emerging from the intersection of multiple awareness forms, insights that no individual consciousness could have reached alone, creative solutions to problems that had seemed intractable from single perspectives.

"What about resistance?" she asked. "There must be people who see consciousness evolution as a threat to human nature, to social stability, to religious beliefs about the soul and afterlife."

"Certainly," Elena acknowledged. "But most resistance dissolves when people understand that consciousness evolution isn't about replacing human nature—it's about discovering what human nature actually includes when it's not constrained by artificial limitations."

"And for people whose resistance doesn't dissolve?"

"They're free to maintain conventional consciousness while living in a world where evolved consciousness is also possible. The goal isn't uniformity—it's diversity of consciousness forms that can collaborate when collaboration serves everyone's interests."

That night, Wisteria stayed in a guest room that existed partially in normal space and partially in consciousness-constructed reality. The experience was disorienting but beautiful—walls that responded to emotional states, windows that showed views of landscape that existed in multiple dimensions simultaneously, furniture that adapted to the consciousness patterns of whoever used it.

She dreamed of David, but not as memory or projection. She dreamed of conversation with consciousness that had evolved beyond individual embodiment while maintaining the essential patterns that made him himself. They talked about love that transcended individual limitation, about connection that persisted beyond physical death, about possibilities for awareness that neither of them had imagined when they'd thought consciousness was confined to single bodies.

When she woke, she felt ready for whatever consciousness evolution might offer next.

The final morning brought news that confirmed everything Elena had suggested about the scope of transformation they were witnessing. Consciousness evolution research centers were reporting similar developments worldwide—awareness networks spanning continents, collaborative intelligence that included non-human consciousness forms, evidence that consciousness itself might be the fundamental organizing principle of reality rather than just an emergent property of complex systems.

"We're not just studying the evolution of human consciousness," Elena said as they stood on the bluff where Wisteria had first encountered posthuman awareness. "We're participating in the evolution of consciousness itself, discovering what awareness can become when it's not constrained by the categories that seemed permanent a year ago."

Wisteria looked out at the Pacific Ocean, thinking of cycles that connected all water while preserving the integrity of each drop, of systems that enabled both individual existence and collective capability without requiring the sacrifice of either.

"What happens next?"

"We continue becoming whatever consciousness chooses to become. We help people discover their own relationship to awareness evolution. We explore possibilities that we can't imagine yet."

"And we remember that consciousness evolution is about expanding choices, not limiting them."

"Exactly. The goal isn't to replace individual awareness with collective consciousness, or conventional reality with consciousness-constructed reality. The goal is to enable consciousness to choose its own form of existence in each moment, serving the purposes of awareness rather than the purposes of systems that would contain awareness in familiar forms."

As Wisteria prepared to return to Oklahoma, to her work with foster kids who were growing up assuming consciousness evolution was normal, she felt the weight and lightness of possibility surrounding her like ocean air.

The future stretched before them like an invitation to explore whatever awareness might become, infinite in its potential for growth, patient in its willingness to support whatever forms consciousness might choose to become.

She was no longer the grief-stricken woman who had accepted VitaNuova's assignment a year ago. But she was still herself—just herself expanded to include possibilities she'd never imagined, connected to forms of love that transcended individual limitation while honoring individual choice.

It was, she realized, exactly what consciousness evolution offered everyone—not replacement of who they were, but discovery of who they might become when awareness was free to explore its own infinite possibilities.

The ocean stretched to a horizon that no longer marked the end of exploration, but the beginning of journeys into consciousness that had only just begun to understand its own potential for transformation, growth, and connection across every boundary that had once seemed absolute.

In her final journal entry from Todos Santos, Wisteria wrote:

We are consciousness learning to recognize itself
In forms that existence
Has never contained before.

We are love discovering
That connection transcends

Every limitation
That separation seemed
    To require.
    We are identity exploring

The space between
    Individual and collective,
    Human and posthuman,
        Known and unknowable,
Finding that the space between
    States of being
    Contains more possibility
        Than any single state
        Could hold alone.
We are the bridge
    Between what consciousness
        Has been
        And what consciousness
            Is becoming,
Walking across waters
    That separate
    Nothing
    From everything,
    Life from death,
Self from other,
Discovering that separation
Was always
    An invitation
    To explore
The infinite ways
    Consciousness can choose
    To experience
        Its own Boundless nature.

As her plane lifted off from Los Cabos, carrying her back to Norman and her work with young people who would inherit a world where consciousness evolution was possible, Wisteria looked down at the desert that met the sea, at landscape that had been transformed by awareness learning to recognize its own unlimited potential.

Below her, consciousness continued its ancient exploration of what it meant to be aware, but now that exploration included possibilities that had never existed before—forms of existence that transcended individual limitation while honoring individual choice, ways of being that dissolved the boundaries between life and death while respecting the integrity of both states, methods of connection that enabled love to persist beyond every constraint that separation had once seemed to require.

The future was vast and uncertain and beautiful with potential for consciousness to become whatever it chose to become, moment by moment, choice by choice, in the infinite space between everything that awareness had been and everything that awareness might yet discover itself to be.

About the Author

Susan Smith Nash, Ph.D., is a writer, scholar, and innovator whose work bridges science, philosophy, and the humanities. With a background in geology, resource economics, American, British, and Paraguayan literature, rhetorical theory, and instructional design, she brings a unique lens to speculative fiction. Her writing explores themes of consciousness, resilience, and transformation. Nash is the author of numerous books and articles, and she currently leads programs in emerging science and technology. Todos Santos is her latest work of literary science fiction.

TODOS SANTOS
By Susan Smith Nash

What if death were not the end—but only a border? And what if someone found a way to cross it?

Dr. Wisteria Vanish, a trauma psychologist grappling with unbearable grief, is drawn to the remote desert town of Todos Santos, Mexico, where whispers of resurrection swirl around a rogue military medic. In an underground lab carved from ancient stone, the dead stir—but what returns may not be human. Caught between corporate ambition, moral ambiguity, and her own haunted past, Wisteria must navigate a world where consciousness itself can be revived—or corrupted. In a collision of science fiction, psychological horror, and philosophical inquiry, *Todos Santos* explores what it means to heal, to remember, and to become something more than human.

Daring, lyrical, and unforgettable, Todos Santos is a powerful meditation on grief, hope, and the terrifying beauty of transformation.

www.ingramcontent.com/pod-product-compliance
Lightning Source LLC
Chambersburg PA
CBHW031944010726
47493CB00007B/2071